JAWS!

Frank and Joe swam on, faster now. Soon Joe spotted another white marker lying in the sand. Apparently, someone knows—or thinks he knows—where the sunken treasure really is, he observed. And that someone is keeping it a secret.

Joe caught Frank's eye and pointed to his watch. They'd told Gina they'd be down only twenty minutes on the first dive, and they'd been down twenty-five already.

Though he hated to tear himself away from the trail of sonar, Frank gave Joe the okay sign. He raised his eyes to the tether Joe held in his hand—and felt as though his heart had stopped beating!

Frank reached out slowly, grabbed Joe's shoulder, and began shaking it.

Puzzled, Joe followed Frank's finger pointing up.

Circling down upon them, with its jaws agape, was an enormous shark!

Books in THE HARDY BOYS CASEFILES® Series

Available from ARCHWAY Paperbacks

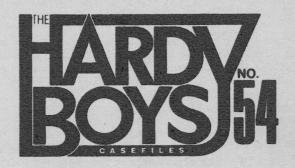

DEEP TROUBLE

FRANKLIN W. DIXON

AN ARCHWAY PAPERBACK
Published by POCKET BOOKS

New York   London   Toronto   Sydney   Tokyo   Singapore

AN ARCHWAY PAPERBACK *Original*

An Archway Paperback published by
POCKET BOOKS, a division of Simon & Schuster Inc.
1230 Avenue of the Americas, New York, NY 10020

Copyright © 1991 by Simon & Schuster Inc.
Produced by Mega-Books of New York, Inc.

ISBN: 0-671-73090-8

First Archway Paperback printing August 1991

10 9 8 7 6 5 4 3 2 1

THE HARDY BOYS, AN ARCHWAY PAPERBACK and colophon are registered trademarks of Simon & Schuster Inc.

THE HARDY BOYS CASEFILES is a trademark of Simon & Schuster Inc.

Cover art by Brian Kotzky

Printed in the U.S.A.

IL 6+

Chapter

1

"YOU CALL THIS a hard diving session? It's been a snap!" Joe Hardy said as he surfaced in the water of Bayport Cove and pulled off his scuba mask.

Joe grinned up at his diving instructor, Dan Fields, and the two men standing with him on the deck of Dan's eighteen-foot inboard, the *Sea Maid*. It was hard to see against the bright summer sky, but it looked as if they were grinning, too.

Just then Joe's brother, Frank, surfaced behind him. Frank, a year older, an inch taller, but sporting ten pounds less of muscle than his brother, pulled off his mask and made a thumbs-up sign at the boat. "Twenty underwater signals completed," he said. "And perfectly interpreted."

1

Treading water, Joe held up the waterproof pad on which he'd written Frank's silent underwater commands. It was a basic scuba-diving exercise, and Frank and Joe had practiced it many times the previous summer. In fact, Frank had been surprised when Dan asked them to prove to his guests that they were fluent in underwater sign language.

"We know this stuff backward and forward," Frank heard Joe brag as the two of them breast-stroked toward the ladder leading to the boat's deck. "How about something a little tougher?"

Dan chuckled, glancing at the two other men. Dan could have been a model for an ad for suntan lotion, Frank decided. His blond hair was in striking contrast to the deep brown of his face and arms. At twenty-two, Dan was only four years older than Frank. He'd started his Bayport scuba-diving school only a year before, but already business was booming.

"So you think you're getting too good for this class, huh?" Dan remarked with a smile. "Well, maybe these guys can offer you a challenge."

"Yeah, who are you two, anyway?" Joe joked as he followed Frank up the ladder. "I mean, I know you're Dr. Benjamin Wills." He nodded to the young, sandy-haired man on Dan's right, who smiled affably in return.

"And you're Harry Lyman." Joe acknowledged the doctor's dark, nervous-looking companion. Harry was about the Hardys' ages, but

2

he had a tight, wiry build and a streetwise attitude, as though he'd grown up in a big city. "But I still don't know what you're doing here watching a scuba lesson."

"Just wanted to see you perform, Joe," said Dr. Wills, handing the younger Hardy a towel. "And I have to say, we weren't disappointed. You two are competent divers."

"Competent?" Frank started to smile and glanced at his younger brother expectantly.

"We're not competent, we're great!" Joe said, getting the laugh from his brother that he expected.

Frank watched as Dan's two guests sized them up, standing there dripping water on the teakwood deck. Dressed in khaki trousers, T-shirts, and deck shoes, the men resembled talent scouts more than the medical doctor and professional diver that Dan had assured him they were. Something was up, Frank knew. It was about time they found out what.

Finally Dr. Wills nodded, satisfied. "We'll have to give them physicals, of course," he said to Dan. "But I think they'll do."

Joe turned to Dan. "What's going on here?"

"Okay, okay." Dan held his hands up and chuckled. "I didn't want to tell you guys in case it didn't work out, but Dr. Wills and Harry are working on a special project in the Bahamas."

"The Bahamas!" Joe exclaimed.

Frank glanced at his brother. He could tell Joe

was jumping to some pretty glamorous conclusions. "What kind of special project?" Frank asked.

"Treasure hunting," Harry said. "We're after the wreck of the *Doña Bonita,* a Spanish galleon that went down in a hurricane in 1625. According to the records, it sank carrying about forty tons of gold and silver from mines in Mexico."

"Forty tons!" Joe's eyes widened. "Just lying on the ocean floor?"

"It's not that easy, Joe." Dr. Wills leaned against the rail of the deck, smiling. "Hundreds of years of storms, shifting sands, barnacles, and corrosion have buried the treasure even deeper."

He stared out at the calm waters of Bayport Cove as though the ocean water might reveal something to him. "Captain Delaney, who heads our project, found evidence two years ago that the ship went down in forty to sixty feet of water off West End on Grand Bahama Island. Since then, he's gone out on search expeditions three times. Until now he's come up empty."

"Until now?"

Harry's lip curled at Joe's obvious eagerness. "We've been out five weeks already on this trip. Last week, using metal detectors, we turned up some ballast stones, and according to the lab tests, they *could* have been on the *Doña Bonita.* It isn't a sure thing, but maybe the cargo is still in the area."

"I don't understand," Joe said. "What's so important about ballast stones?"

"They're not really stones," Harry said in a superior voice. "Back then, ballast stones were made of iron. They were carried on ships to balance or steady them." He gave the Hardys a condescending look. "Ballast stones and cargo are usually all that's left of a wooden ship after three hundred years under water."

"But wait, there's something I don't get," said Frank, turning to Dr. Wills. "You're a medical doctor, right? What's a doctor doing hunting for treasure?"

"Diving for treasure is dangerous business," Dr. Wills said evenly. "Every operation needs a medic on board in case a diver gets the bends or loses oxygen while he's under. And there are plenty of injuries, believe me. Captain Delaney and I have been friends for years. He knows I share his enthusiasm for sunken treasure, and he took me on the last two expeditions. Harry's our best diver. Of course, I have to dive, too—everyone does on these small operations."

"Especially since if you dive, you share in the profits," Harry added.

"So that brings us to you two," Dr. Wills concluded, straightening up again. "Dan, whose opinion I highly respect, tells me you're his star pupils. We're looking for someone to hire."

Frank was surprised. "But you've been out

for five weeks already. Don't you have a full crew?''

Dr. Wills cast his eyes down. "We lost one of our divers—Peter Duvall," he said. "We figured we could make do without a replacement, but now that there's a really good chance of cashing in, Captain Delaney wants to step up the search and expand the crew.''

"So you want us to dive for treasure?" Joe's eyes were gleaming in anticipation. "This is too good to be true."

"Hold on, little brother." Frank flashed Joe a warning glance. "First we'd better find out what happened to Peter Duvall. I have a feeling Dad's going to want to know."

"Well, we can't tell you." Harry eyed Frank so defiantly that the older Hardy felt suspicious. "He just disappeared. Left the ship one day after a dive and never showed up again.''

Frank pondered this. It sounded strange, he told himself, but at least the guy hadn't had a diving accident. That should make their father happy. "Why us?" he asked suspiciously.

"Why not?" Dr. Wills was beginning to look impatient, and Frank noted Joe's alarmed reaction. "We've already hired a marine archaeology student from Florida. Her name's Gina Daniels. She had flooded us with letters begging us to let her crew on the *Valiant*. Her résumé's great, and she's a decent diver, too. All we need now are two more divers and we're set.''

Frank glanced at Dan, whose nod told Frank that it seemed like a good deal to him. Still, something about Harry's attitude made Frank wonder if there was something the two men weren't telling them.

"Wow, that's great!" Joe said, shaking Dr. Wills's hand. "Good thing school's out. When do we leave?"

"First"—Dr. Wills smiled—"I want to see you dive with our equipment. Harry'll go down with you to see how you do."

"Fine with us," Joe said before Frank could open his mouth.

Frank's eyes widened as he watched Harry unload the expedition gear from a locker on deck.

"Nothing small-time about this operation," Frank acknowledged.

"No way." Joe whistled. "This stuff is state-of-the-art." He squatted down to inspect one of the buoyancy control jackets. "Get a load of this BC jacket," he said. "It's even got zippered pockets for extra weights and a pressure valve for adding air, all in one neat package."

"So, you want to give it a try?" Dr. Wills asked, but Frank could see he already knew the answer.

Balancing on the slightly rolling deck, Frank, Joe, and Harry donned the leggings, BC jackets, and other paraphernalia. Dan and Dr. Wills helped them secure the straps on their air tanks.

7

"How deep was their last dive?" the doctor asked Dan Fields.

Dan checked his clipboard. "Forty feet."

"How about taking it to sixty?" Dr. Wills suggested.

"Whatever you say." Dan slipped out of his khakis, revealing swimming trunks underneath. Then he raised the boat's anchor and started the engine. Meanwhile, Frank and Joe methodically tested their air hoses, mouthpieces, and pressure gauges. Everything seemed in order.

"This looks like a good spot," Frank heard Dan call out as the engine rumbled to a stop.

"Wow, cool fins even," Joe said as he and Frank strapped them on. After they were completely dressed, Dr. Wills approached them with a clipboard.

"Here are five tasks I want you to perform in this order," he said, handing them a sheet of plasticized paper. "You'll be able to read them underwater with your head lamps."

Frank peered over Joe's shoulder at the large type. The tasks looked pretty standard: entry, descent, hovering over the floor of the bay without disturbing the site, signaling successfully to each other, and finally ascending to the surface. Frank knew that he and Joe had practiced this process many times. He felt confident that they'd do fine. "When do we start?" he asked.

"You already have." Dr. Wills marked several boxes on his clipboard. "You get top points for setting up and checking your gear correctly."

He glanced at Harry, who was just strapping on his fins. "Okay, we're all set. Over the side, and good luck down there."

Frank and Joe backed up against the railing and easily flipped over into the water. Frank knew they'd earn extra points for making perfect entries. Those were important when it was necessary to disturb a diving site as little as possible. In the water, he and Joe adjusted the valves on their BC jackets, releasing air, which allowed them to sink slowly.

Underwater, the light was a beautiful deep blue, growing to a deeper, richer color as the boys sank to the flat, sandy bottom of the bay. Frank wondered what the Caribbean must look like sixty feet down as he glanced up to see Harry slip through the surface above them. The sun glistening on the water turned Harry's body into a silhouette as he, too, slowly sank.

Items one and two were almost taken care of, Frank told himself. Number three was to "hover" over the sandy floor. Frank fine-tuned the valve on his BC jacket, letting out just enough air so he didn't sink too fast and disturb the site. They were approaching a depth of forty feet, and Frank could just make out the bottom of the bay twenty feet below.

At sixty feet Frank faced Joe, barely two feet

above the bottom. They snapped on their head lamps, enjoying the extended view.

Sure hope Harry's taking notes, Frank thought, proud of his and Joe's efforts.

Not a speck of sand rose to disturb the site. Frank knew this was a sign of expert diving.

As Harry reached their depth, Frank noted that he, too, hovered over the bottom without effort. Frank moved toward Joe to check the list of signals they were to give, but as he tried to read the list, Joe's hands began to jerk in spasms.

Frank pulled back to see what was wrong with Joe. At first it was hard to read his expression through the mask. But then Joe's hands went to his throat in the universal signal for scuba divers.

Joe was signaling that he had no air!

Quickly Frank checked Joe's pressure gauge. It still read Full, as it should have. Confused, Frank turned to Harry for assistance. But Harry seemed frozen in place.

Frank's head was spinning as he checked his brother, whose signals were becoming more frantic. Frank forced himself to stay calm so he could think through the emergency procedures Dan had taught him.

He had to do something *now!*

Chapter

2

AIR!

Joe tried to scream as he grabbed at his throat. From somewhere deep inside came a warning not to panic, but his hands wanted to claw at his face mask and his lungs felt as if they were about to burst. He vaguely realized that someone was moving around him. He struck out at the moving figure, desperate for air.

The figure was Frank! Finally, through his oxygenless haze, Joe realized that his brother was offering him his own mouthpiece.

Air! Gratefully, Joe crammed the mouthpiece into his mouth and drew in a cool, sweet stream of air.

That was close. Joe closed his eyes, waiting for the dizziness to pass and realized that he was covered with sweat inside his scuba outfit. After another breath he handed the mouthpiece back to Frank. The two brothers passed Frank's mouthpiece back and forth as they swam back to the surface.

By the time he reached the ladder, Joe was fighting mad. The grim expression on Frank's face told Joe he felt the same way.

"What's going on?" Frank demanded as the two boys planted themselves, dripping, on deck.

Joe, too, wanted an explanation. He threw off his face mask and faced Harry, who had climbed up the ladder behind them.

"My air was cut off," Joe told him, red-faced. "And I don't think it was an accident!"

"Hey, wait a minute!" Dan cried, stepping between the two. "What happened?"

"Hey, guys." Harry paled at Dan's shocked reaction. "It was just a test, to see how you'd handle an emergency. That's a training tank, set to cut off the air supply at sixty feet. I could have hit a release button to turn the air back on if I'd had to. You were in no danger."

Dan and Frank stared at him in shocked silence. Joe slipped out of the air tank and tossed it, with his face mask, angrily into the footlocker.

"I had no idea they were planning t-this—" Dan stammered.

"Don't worry about it," Joe growled. "If they try anything like that again, I'll flatten them."

A hard look came into Harry's narrow brown eyes as he returned Joe's icy stare.

"All right. I apologize," Dr. Wills said tentatively. "We needed to know how you'd react in a real emergency. On a dive, our lives could depend on your reflexes."

He took a deep breath. "The good news is, you passed the test," he added. "We're willing to take you on for the remaining two weeks of our current set of dives. If you want the job, it's yours."

Joe hesitated. He was now suspicious of these two strangers.

Then, grudgingly, he took the doctor's hand and shook it.

"We don't pay much up front," the doctor said, obviously relieved, "but we all share in the profits if we come up with the goods."

Now that he'd shaken on it, Joe started to feel more optimistic. He checked out his brother's reaction and saw that Frank was still suspicious. "We'll think about it," Frank said firmly. "We'll have to talk it over with our parents. Is there somewhere we can contact you tomorrow?"

"Harry and I are flying back in my two-seater tomorrow morning," the doctor said.

He pulled out a business card and scribbled something on the back of it. "Call me at this number. If you decide to go, I'll leave a couple of tickets for you at the airport before I leave."

"This is pretty quick," Joe said, taking the card.

"That's the way we operate." The sandy-haired doctor flashed a grin at the boys. "Rough and ready, and determined to win."

That night at dinner Joe wished his father was a little less determined.

"Absolutely not," Fenton Hardy said as he passed the mashed potatoes to Joe. "I've never heard of this Dr. Wills or Harry Lyman. And we agreed that this summer you boys would forget about work and concentrate on having good, all-American fun."

"But what could be more fun than diving for sunken treasure?" Joe protested through a mouthful of roast beef. His mother, Laura Hardy, frowned at him until he clamped his mouth shut and chewed.

Fenton sighed, exchanging a glance with his wife. Joe was sure his father understood their enthusiasm. Fenton himself was a famous detective, and as far as Joe knew he'd never turned down a case or anything adventurous.

"How long is it for?" he asked again.

"Two weeks, Dad. Like tennis camp! We'll be back before you know it. Who knows, maybe we'll have enough gold to sail back on our own yacht!"

"Over my dead body," Laura snapped, but Joe noticed that she had an amused smile on her face. That was a good sign. Joe crossed his fingers under the table. He had a feeling they were going to say yes.

Fenton wiped his mouth with his napkin and sighed. "All right," he said at last. "I'll check Captain Delaney out. If he's clean, you boys can go.

"But—" he added quickly before Joe could jump up from the table, "I want your word that there's no mystery involved in this."

His words stopped Joe in midleap. Sinking down in his chair again, he exchanged a glance with his brother.

"No, sir." Joe coughed nervously. "Nothing that I can think of."

Joe listened to the clock tick in the nearby foyer as his mother and father eyed him skeptically. Well, it wasn't a lie, he told himself. Peter Duvall just got fed up and quit the operation—right?

Finally Fenton rose from the table. Joe's eyes met his brother's. They had done it. The next day they'd be on their way to the Bahamas!

"Wow, look at that!" Joe nudged Frank as their plane circled a collection of emerald-colored islands set like a strand of jewels in a turquoise sea. "Can you tell which one we're going to land on?"

"Try the one with the airport," Frank said, shaking his head at his younger brother's eagerness. "Remember what Dad said when he dropped us off. This Captain Delaney has a record of leading wild-goose chases. After twenty years of hunting treasure, he still owes money on his boat. Don't lose your head while you dream of getting rich."

"Yeah, yeah." Joe buckled his seat belt in preparation for landing. "Tell you what, Frank. You take care of the sensible attitude on this trip. I just want to have fun. Bahamas, here I come!"

As they departed the plane and entered the two-story airport with its five departure gates Joe remarked, "Hey, it looks like the airport in Bayport."

"Except Bayport was never this crowded. What's going on?" Frank scanned the milling crowds that filled the building outside the customs area. Then he pointed to a gaily painted banner hanging on a far wall. It read First International Speedboat Races, August 7–13.

"All right! That's this week!" Joe lifted their bags onto a custom official's counter. "If we have next Sunday off, maybe we can go."

Joe's enthusiasm was interrupted by a somber-looking customs official in a trim blue suit, who was gesturing impatiently toward something in Frank's bag. "Excuse me," he said in a clipped Bahamian accent that sounded almost British. "Would you explain what this is, please?"

"Sure." Frank lifted out a black plastic box

and held it out for the official to see. "It's a portable depth gauge. It works by sonar. You just hit this button and—"

Joe was impatient. "Look, if it'll cause a delay, just keep it until our return flight," he told the official.

"A depth gauge?" The inspector looked at the box suspiciously.

"We're crewing aboard a salvage ship just off the island," Frank explained.

"Oh. The *Valiant?*" The official became instantly interested and more relaxed, too, Joe noticed. "I've read about it in the papers. You boys are new on board?"

"Yes, sir." Joe tried to be polite, but he was itching to get out of the airport. "Today's our first day. I sure hope we won't be late."

The inspector smiled, pasted some stickers on the boys' suitcases, and waved them on. "If you find treasure, bring some gold for me!" he joked.

As the Hardys headed for the glass exit doors, Joe felt the excitement of being in a foreign country. The tropical breeze and warm sun that greeted them as they stepped outside made him glad that he and Frank had decided to come.

"Look," Joe said, pointing to a person in a cap a short distance away. The figure held a sign that read *Valiant*. "He must be here to take us to the boat."

As the brothers headed toward the person, Joe waved his arm to get his attention. Just as they reached him, the person turned suddenly and banged into Joe's arm.

"We— Oh!" Joe stared at the young woman in front of him. Her cap had been knocked off, sending a shower of blond hair down her back. Joe laughed, embarrassed. "Sorry. I thought you were a guy. I guess the way your hair was piled up under there, I—"

"Don't worry about it." The woman, tanned and freckle faced beneath her lion's mane of hair, smiled in a friendly way at the brothers. "I've been called worse in my life. You're Joe, I take it. Or is it Frank?"

"I'm Joe. He's Frank. And you're—?" Still a little embarrassed, Joe retrieved the woman's cap and handed it to her. She had a low, throaty voice that appealed to him.

"Gina Daniels. I'm on the crew. I volunteered to take you guys out to the ship. Ready?"

"Uh, sure." Joe followed Gina through the parking lot to a dark green hatchback. He caught Frank's amused glance and flushed dark red. He knew what Frank was thinking. Gina was the marine archaeologist Dr. Wills had mentioned. That meant she must be at least eight years older than he was.

Oh, well, he thought wistfully as he and Frank threw their bags into the back of the car. I haven't considered older women before, but there's always a first time.

Besides, Gina looked younger than twenty-five. She revved the car's engine as Frank climbed into the backseat and Joe took the seat beside her. "I can't believe the crowds today," she said as they started off along a narrow asphalt road that led through Freeport and out among flat, green hills dotted with restaurants, resorts, and private homes. "This is the first year they've had a motorboat race on the island. The big events are usually held on Nassau."

"Yeah, we were hoping to watch it," Joe commented. "So tell me, what's it like aboard the *Valiant?*" he asked, changing the subject. "Are you the only woman on the ship?"

"Yep," she said simply. "I have a cabin there, but I've also rented a little apartment on land. Captain Delaney, Dr. Wills, and the rest of the crew live on board ship full-time."

"Did you know that diver Peter Duvall?" Frank asked from the backseat. "We're supposed to be replacing him."

Joe watched as Gina dropped her carefree expression as quickly as she would a paper mask. She darted a glance in his direction, then turned her attention to the road once more.

"No, he was gone by the time I signed on," she said with feigned carelessness. Neither of the Hardys was fooled.

"Didn't mean to upset you," Frank ventured.

"It's all right. I'm fine." Gina blinked. "It's just that I don't think he took off on his own the way everyone says he did."

Joe was startled by the anger in her voice. "You want to tell us what you do think?" he suggested gently.

Gina hesitated. Then she took her eyes off the road to meet his eyes directly for a minute. "I have a confession to make," she said. "I volunteered to pick you up so I could talk to you."

"But you don't even know us," Joe protested.

Gina smiled grimly. "Last year my aunt who lives in New Hampshire suspected that her business partner was misusing company funds. She contacted a private investigator—your father. When I met him you were all he talked about. You're investigators, too, right?"

"Sometimes," Frank admitted. "But we've been hired to work on this dive."

"I understand, but I have to talk to someone about this," she said. "Please, you have to help." She blinked, fighting back tears as she waited for the boys to respond.

"Whatever it is, we'll do all we can," Joe assured her. "What's the trouble?"

"There's danger on board the *Valiant*," Gina said in her throaty voice. "Every person involved in this treasure hunt could be in danger."

Joe stared at her, stunned. But before he could say anything, he noticed something strange about the scenery. He glanced up, and his eyes widened.

A small dog had run out into the road, directly in front of Gina's car!

"Watch out!" Frank called from the backseat.

Gina cried out as she swerved to avoid the cringing dog.

The hatchback careened into the opposite lane, where a truck sped toward them at about sixty-five miles per hour.

"We're going to crash!" Horns blared and brakes screeched as Joe automatically shielded his head with his arms. Bravely Gina fought with the spinning steering wheel.

But the car continued on its collision course, straight toward that speeding truck!

Chapter

3

"LET UP on the brake!" Frank gripped the back of the front seat as Joe grabbed the steering wheel from Gina and turned it sharply to the left. The tires screeched against the asphalt as the car spun in a half circle until it was facing in the opposite direction. Frank watched, horrified, as the truck, which also swerved, missed them by scant inches.

"That was close." The car had stalled and was halfway on the shoulder but to Frank's relief they were safe. Down the road, the driver of the beat-up pickup truck they'd nearly hit gave a honk and a casual wave as he drove out of sight.

"Welcome to the Bahamas," Joe said weakly. He reached for Gina's hand. "Are you all right?"

From the backseat, Frank could see that Gina was still trembling. "We might have all been killed," she said. "I'm sorry—"

Shaken, the three young people got out of the hatchback and stood gazing out at the bright ocean. The gentle rolling of the waves soothed them, and after a while Joe asked tentatively, "You were saying you think we're all in danger?"

Gina took a deep breath. "I'm going to tell you something I haven't told anyone here. I went after this job for a special reason. My last name is Daniels," she said, "but my stepfather's last name is Duvall. Peter is his son and my half-brother, and I want to know where he is."

So there was a mystery here, after all. "You think someone might have hurt him?" Frank asked.

Gina turned to him. "Peter and I were very close. He wrote me just about every week. His last letter hinted that something weird was happening on board the ship."

"Have you learned anything since you've been on board?" Joe asked.

"Only that Captain Delaney has sunk his last dime into this project and is starting to run scared," she said. "He's working the crew until they drop."

"But could that have anything to do with your brother's disappearance?" Frank asked.

"I don't know what to think anymore. That's

why I was so happy to hear you guys were showing up. I need your help badly," she said.

"Okay," Joe said after a moment. "We'll make a deal. We won't tell anyone who you really are if you don't tell anyone about our detective work. Deal?"

"Does that mean you'll help?" she asked hopefully.

"We'll do all we can," Frank said. "Right now we have to get going—they're waiting for us. You'd better let me drive the rest of the way."

Minutes later Frank maneuvered the car into the lot at West End's rustic marina. He switched off the engine and stared at the row of boats moored beside a wooden walkway that lined the shore.

"The *Valiant!*" Joe whistled in approval as he got out of the car, keeping his eyes on the forty-foot salvage ship moored there. It was freshly painted, and its white exterior gleamed pink in the light from the setting sun.

"Captain Delaney bought it at auction from the Coast Guard," Gina explained. "Fixed it up all by himself, too. But it's the crew members who keep it shipshape."

"A regular yacht," Frank joked as he retrieved their bags. He followed Gina and Joe up the gangplank to the deck.

"Welcome aboard!"

Frank set the bags down to take the hand of a bearded, bare-chested, middle-aged man in Bermuda shorts and deck shoes. "I'm Captain Delaney. You know Dr. Wills here, I believe."

"Pleased to meet you, Captain." Frank shook his hand. Delaney looked more like a beachcomber than Frank's idea of a ship's captain.

"Glad you boys could make it," Dr. Wills said as Joe shook hands with the captain. "Now maybe we can get some solid work done."

Frank eyed the doctor carefully. He seemed more tense than he had in Bayport. Frank wondered if something was wrong with the project. "Where do we stow these?" he asked, gesturing toward the bags.

"I'll show you." Delaney led them to the deck. "Then you can meet the rest of the crew."

As he and Joe followed the captain, Frank spotted Harry Lyman just ahead of them, talking with a tall, lean, red-haired crew member who appeared to be about eighteen. Harry was leaning against the outer wall of the cabin, telling an animated story to his crewmate, but he stopped midsentence when he saw the Hardys. A hard, surly expression took over his face.

"Ah, Harry!" the captain said. "You've met Frank and Joe, haven't you? Why don't you show them to their quarters?" He turned to the Hardys. "I hope you understand. Sunday is the crew's day off, but with what I've got riding on this project I don't dare take an extra hour off."

25

"Thanks, Captain." Joe said. "We'll get our stuff stowed in a jiffy."

"I'm Frank Hardy," his brother said to the other crew member in the meantime, shaking the redhead's hand. "This is my brother, Joe. We're the new divers replacing Peter Duvall."

"Vic Chapin. Good to meet you." Vic had the open and easygoing manner of someone from a small town. "Glad to have more help around here for a change."

"Come on, guys, if you're coming," Harry said impatiently, heading for the companionway leading two levels down to the living quarters. "People can't stand around jawing on this ship."

Yeah, except for you, Frank thought as they squeezed down the narrow companionway to the passageway below. He wasn't surprised by Harry's attitude, though. Even after only one meeting he was almost used to it.

The passageway was lined with cabins, and Harry stopped in front of one of them.

"You're in cabins six and seven, right next to mine," Harry told them. "Keys are in the doors."

Frank dumped his gear and was surprised at how nice his room was, with wood paneling, a bunk, closet, and even a writing desk.

"What's yours like?" Frank called to his brother, who had moved on down the corridor.

"A mirror image of yours," he heard Joe call back.

"Ten cabins and a head at either end of the hall," Harry told them. "With Gina aboard, we'll still have one cabin vacant. If Peter shows up again I guess they'll give it to him."

"How long ago did he disappear?"

"Sunday before last. Two weeks ago exactly." Harry eyed him thoughtfully. "Why are you asking?"

"I wondered what happened to him, that's all," said Frank.

Harry shrugged. "Maybe he found a chunk of gold and just took off, who knows? Or maybe he just got tired of working so hard." His nervous laugh sounded more like hiccups. "Look, guys, I love chatting with you, but we better get topside before Delaney starts squawking."

Frank and Joe locked their rooms and followed Harry upstairs. "This is where we eat," Harry announced as they passed a doorway. "We use it as a lounge, too, on the few occasions when we don't have to work."

Frank peeked inside. The room was small but comfortably furnished with a large round table in the center, low bookshelves loaded with magazines, and a few overstuffed easy chairs.

"Bob, I wondered where you were." At the sound of Harry's greeting, Frank checked out the stocky, jovial-looking man approaching them. Though he couldn't have been more than twenty-two, he was out of shape and could barely squeeze through the narrow passageway.

Frank wondered how he managed to dive for gold.

"I was just going to play some cards with Vic. Want to join us?" the man asked.

"Bob Fowler, Frank and Joe Hardy." Harry turned sideways so Bob could reach past him to shake hands. "They're the new guys on board, and, no, I don't know where Vic is. I've got better stuff to do on my day off than play gin rummy with you guys."

"Well, excu-use me!" Bob said with a grin.

Frank heard a clattering on the companionway behind Bob.

"Ah!" the portly crew member said. "Sounds like Poison! Our former cook and only native Bahamian."

"You said it, man." A young man appeared on the stairs. His dark skin was in stark contrast to his white shirt and slacks. Frank enjoyed his pleasant Bahamian accent. "Poison's just a nickname, of course." He grinned at the Hardys. "They don't let me cook much for them anymore. These days, I just dive. Anyway, feel free to call me Alastair."

"A real Bahamian?" Joe shook his hand. "You mean you've lived in this paradise all your life?"

"All my life? No, not yet."

Everyone laughed as Harry, Frank, and Joe went up the companionway and Alastair and Vic squeezed into the lounge. Frank and Joe were still smiling when they surfaced and found the captain staring out at the horizon as the last of the sun's rays turned the calm water pink and then red. He was lost in thought.

"Ah, that sweet Caribbean air," Joe said, taking a deep breath. "And tons of gold beneath us. All we need now are a few more divers of the female persuasion—"

The captain whirled around and faced them in the near dark with such a dour expression that Joe froze in midsentence. "I expect everyone to be ready on deck at dawn tomorrow," he said sharply, ignoring Joe. "Harry, you'll be paired with Joe Hardy. I'm going to my cabin now. I suggest you do the same."

Frank stared after the captain. Delaney's expression had aroused his curiosity. Was Delaney anxious about the sunken treasure? Or about Peter Duvall?

"What'd I say?" Joe asked, holding his hands out helplessly.

"Only thing to do when he gets like that," Alastair said, appearing from nowhere with a plate of sandwiches, "is to keep out of sight. I suggest we have something to eat."

"I'll take one. Thanks," Joe said, reaching for a sandwich. "As long as you didn't make them."

"If I did, I'm not telling," Alastair replied.

As Joe reached for a sandwich, Frank's eye caught the gleam of a handsome gold signet ring on Alastair's hand. "Great ring," he said. "Did you get that on the island?"

Alastair flinched so suddenly he almost dropped the plate. But he recovered quickly. "No, actually I don't know where it's from," he said with a smile. "It's been in the family for years."

He turned away and found Gina standing right behind him. Her eyes were on his ring, and Frank noticed the very strange expression on her face.

"Sandwich?" Alastair said to her as he held out the tray.

Gina jerked back a bit and stared up into his dark brown eyes. "No," she said in a low voice. Then added, "Thank you."

Alastair shrugged and moved past her. Gina, obviously very upset, turned in the opposite direction to lean against the rail and stare out at the dark water just as the captain had earlier.

Frank moved close to her. "Is something wrong?" he asked in a low voice.

Gina grew pale as she spoke the words. "That ring," she murmured. "It was a present last year—from me to my brother!"

Chapter

4

"WHAT'S POISON DOING with your brother's ring?" Frank whispered to Gina.

Gina didn't respond—she just continued to stare at the water.

Joe walked up to the pair. "What do you say we check out the—" He cut himself off as he noticed Gina's expression.

Frank quickly explained what had transpired.

"That sure makes Poison look suspicious," Joe commented after he had heard the story.

"You're right," Frank answered, "but I think we should hit the sack now. I need a good night's sleep to help me fit the pieces in place."

At six o'clock the next morning the alarm jolted Joe out of a very deep sleep. He felt the rumble of the ship's engines. The *Valiant* must already be headed out to the diving site. Joe dressed quickly and walked up the companionway.

"Hey, Joe, in here!" Bob Fowler called as Joe stumbled past the dining room with his eyes still half closed. "You've got to eat before you can dive! We all make our own breakfast here, since Poison turned out to be a bust in the kitchen. Come on, I'll whip you up a fruit salad."

"Thanks." Joe stumbled in to join Bob, Vic, Alastair, Frank, and Gina. "Am I the last one up?"

"Looks like it," Gina said amiably. "Harry and Jason already ate."

"Who's Jason?" Joe fell into an empty chair.

"Jason Matthews—another diver. He pilots the boat, too, so we don't see him much down here. And Harry wanted to get up on deck early to get the diving equipment ready."

"Great." Joe exchanged glances with his brother. "Better make a point of checking the air supply valve, I guess."

"Right," Vic said. "He told me what he did to you guys in Bayport. You've got to watch Harry. He's a moody guy."

Moody isn't the word for it, Joe thought glumly as he climbed on deck half an hour later. The ship was now at anchor and Harry was already climbing into his diving gear. His expression was very grim.

"Something wrong?" Joe asked Harry as

Frank helped secure the air tank on his back. "You look kind of tense."

"I feel fine," Harry snapped. He turned abruptly to the captain and asked, "What's on the agenda for today?"

"You need to take a couple of markers to put at the site of anything important you find," the captain said, nodding toward a case of white metal squares at their feet.

Joe picked up a couple and examined them. They were about ten inches square, and each had a black number painted in its center. Joe noticed that Harry was closely inspecting the markers that the captain handed him.

"Joe, you take charge of the magnetometer," the captain continued, handing it to him. "Whenever it identifies a metallic object, pick the object up and place it in your net bag to bring with you when you surface."

"It looks like a weed cutter." Joe examined the long handle with a circular tube at the end.

"It usually turns up a lot of junk," the captain said. "The U.S. Navy used this area for a dumping ground at one time. But we sort it all out topside after the dive."

"What's that thing?" Frank pointed to a long hose that a dark-haired young man was wrestling over the rail. Joe eyed the guy curiously. He had to be Jason, the diver he hadn't yet met.

"It's called an Air Lift," the young man said shyly. Joe noticed he had a strong Southern accent. "It's a sand vacuum. It clears away debris as divers scan the ocean floor."

"I'm all set, if you're through with the lecture, Jason," Harry interrupted. "Are we going or not?"

Joe eyed his diving partner curiously. Something was up with Harry. He seemed way too nervous for a routine dive. Joe didn't relish the thought of going underwater with him again, but a job was a job "Watch yourself down there," he heard Frank mutter as he moved toward the edge with his gear.

Joe didn't need to be warned. He double-checked the air supply valve on his BC jacket, then backed up to the railing next to Harry, and an instant later splashed horizontally into the clear blue water.

Wow! Joe said to himself as he entered the beautiful underwater world of the Caribbean. Wait till Frank sees this!

Though he was just beneath the surface of the water, he found himself already surrounded by brilliantly colored tropical fish and shafts of shimmering light. This is nothing like Bayport Cove, he thought.

As he and Harry released air from their BC jackets, Joe descended deeper into the underwater spectacle. At forty feet the bottom came into view. Joe realized that he didn't need his head lamp even at that depth. The sun penetrated the clear water and was reflected back by mounds of white and pink coral.

Okay, guy, back to work, Joe told himself sternly. Tearing his eyes away from the amazing scenery, he switched on the magnetometer and began scanning the bottom while Harry followed with the Air Lift hose, waiting for Joe's signal to begin clearing sand and debris.

After probing the area for ten minutes, Joe noticed the red light on the magnetometer flashing. He signaled to Harry to vacuum the area with the Air Lift.

As Joe moved back out of the way, Harry cleared the area with the vacuum. Soon they were able to retrieve the metal object. Eyeglass frames! Joe said to himself. He put them into his net bag as he'd been instructed for inspection on the surface.

An hour later, having half-filled his bag with unexciting metal objects, Joe came upon a large mound that set the magnetometer's light flashing madly. Harry managed to communicate to him that they were some of the ballast stones found earlier. Harry pointed to the markers secured to the mound, but Joe couldn't figure out what he was trying to say.

Shift's over, Joe said to himself as he checked the diver's watch Vic had lent him for the morning. Time to return to the ship. As he signaled Harry, he saw something was wrong.

Harry had dropped the Air Lift hose and was

clutching his side. He seemed to be in terrible pain.

Do something! Joe urged himself, snapping out of his momentary shock. He moved quickly through the water toward his partner, trying to keep his breathing as regular as possible. He peered into Harry's face mask. The young man was pale, and his eyes were half closed. Quickly and efficiently, Joe adjusted the air valves on both their jackets and supported Harry as the two of them rose slowly toward the ship.

"Something's wrong with Harry!" Joe yelled the moment they broke the surface and he was able to rip off both their masks. "Toss down a line. I think you'll have to pull him aboard."

The crew wasted no time springing into action. Bob threw out a line, but Harry seemed to recover a little and waved the line away. "It's okay," he said stoically. "Just some cramps. I'm all right now. Must've eaten too much this morning."

To Joe's surprise, he climbed up the ladder on his own.

"Take it easy," Dr. Wills said as he helped Harry onto the deck. "Lie down. Jason and Alastair, unstrap his air tanks. Vic, get my stethoscope."

Joe watched as the doctor listened to Harry's heartbeat. Wills's expression was grim. Finally he straightened up and said to Harry, "I'm going to help you down to my cabin for a closer look. Gina, come give me a hand."

Gina and Dr. Wills carefully lifted the pale diver and helped him down the companionway to the doctor's quarters, leaving behind a shaken captain to collect the markers that Harry had dropped.

"Return these to the storeroom, will you?" Delaney said to Jason. Joe watched the middle-aged man, feeling sorry for him. "We've got a lot of daylight left," the captain said, steeling himself to go on. "Chapin and Fowler, get into your gear. You're on the next dive detail."

Joe finished removing his gear and accepted a towel from his brother.

"What do you make of this?" Frank asked under his breath.

Joe shrugged, still shaken. "Bad news," he acknowledged. "Could be nothing. But it seems like there's been a whole lot of nothing around here lately."

The crew's morale seemed crushed for the day. That evening, after the last divers had climbed aboard empty-handed and everyone had cleaned up and retired to his cabin, Joe saw Harry pass by his open doorway.

"Hey, Harry!" he called out. "How're you feeling? You had us all worried."

Harry paused and stuck his head in the door. "I'm strong like bull," he boomed in a phony Russian accent. Then he said in a normal voice, "Really, it was just the breakfast. Dr. Wills gave me an antacid. I'm as good as new." He hesitated, then said, "Thanks for taking care of me."

"No problem," Joe said easily. "Though I have to admit, I wondered at first if it was another one of your tests."

"What's all the noise out here?" Frank asked, walking up to Harry. "Hey, I thought you were supposed to be resting."

"Actually, I was wondering," Harry said a little uneasily. "Could you guys come to my cabin for a few minutes? There's something I want to talk to you about."

Joe and Frank both were surprised. Joe followed Frank's gaze and noticed that Harry's left arm was tucked into his right armpit in an odd and awkward way.

"Sure," Joe said to the diver and followed him down the passageway with Frank. But he noticed that Harry's hand trembled as he tried to unlock his cabin door. When the key dropped to the floor, Frank bent to retrieve it.

What could Harry have to tell them? Joe wondered as they followed him inside. Could Harry have something to do with Peter's disappearance?

"Ouch!" Joe said suddenly, stepping back out into the corridor. Then he realized what had attacked him. He held up an ice pick, which had been lying on a shelf near the doorway, the point facing out.

"What's this?" he demanded. "On call for icebergs?" He rubbed his arm where the pick had stabbed him.

Harry was embarrassed. "Sorry," he said. "I always leave the key in the lock outside and end up locking myself in. You need a key to unlock the door from the inside. I got tired of always yelling for help, so I put the pick up there to stick in the opening in the knob. It releases the lock."

"A likely story," Joe joked as Frank pointedly retrieved the key from the outside lock and handed it to Harry.

"You did it again," Frank said.

"See what I mean?" Harry laughed nervously and put the key on the desk.

"So?" Joe demanded, taking the only chair and forcing the others to sit on the bed. "What's the story, Harry? You're being blackmailed by a gang of mermaids or what?"

"This is serious," Harry said with a scowl. "I got this funny feeling. Like something's happening or about to happen on the ship."

"Like what?" Frank asked reasonably.

"Well, first Peter disappears," Harry answered. "Then the captain starts acting like that captain in *The Caine Mutiny*. You know, like the crew's his enemy and he's got to defeat us with twenty-four-hour-a-day work." He shook his head, narrowing his brown eyes. "I think Delaney knows a lot more than he's letting on."

"What do you know about Peter?" Joe asked, studying the diver.

"Nothing much. He was real quiet, always writing things down. Kept to himself a lot, even on our Sundays off."

"You think Captain Delaney got rid of him?" Frank asked.

"Yeah, I do," Harry blurted out. "If by getting rid of him you mean the guy was killed—" To his embarrassment, Harry began to hiccup.

Joe stared at him. "You think Delaney killed Peter Duvall?" he demanded.

"Well, I don't see the guy anywhere, do you?" Harry insisted. "I don't trust Delaney."

"How come you're telling us this?" Joe asked him.

Harry's face fell. "Look, I gotta tell someone," he said in a low voice. "The tension's killing me. I mean, it could be me he goes after next!"

Joe tried to understand what he was saying. "Do you have any proof about the captain?"

Harry shook his head. "Nothing but a hunch. But I'd take a look at those markers they're always so careful about."

"What about them?"

Harry crossed to his closet and took out two of the white markers. "I snitched these last night. Look alike, right?"

Frank took one in each hand. "Yeah. So?"

"Give them a heft. They don't' weigh the same." Harry stepped back, pleased with himself.

Joe watched Frank carefully weigh a marker in each hand, then switch hands and heft them again. "You're right," Frank said. He held up one of the markers. "This one's definitely heavier."

"So what?" Joe said impatiently. "What's it got to do with the captain?"

"I'm coming to that," Harry said, getting excited and beginning to pace back and forth across the tiny room. "I think I got it figured. I only told one other person about this, but—"

"Who else did you tell?" Joe cut in.

"I told—" But Harry was unable to finish the sentence.

As Joe watched in horror, Harry's face flushed red, then purple. The diver screamed and clutched at his heart. Panic-stricken, he turned to each of the brothers in turn, then collapsed facedown on the floor.

"Not again!" Joe yelled as both brothers rushed to the fallen body. Frank grabbed Harry's wrist and checked for a pulse, while Joe pressed a finger against the diver's jugular vein.

"Feel anything?" he asked his brother.

Incredulous, Frank shook his head. "Nothing," he said in a low voice.

The brothers stared down at what had been Harry Lyman. He had died before their very eyes!

Chapter

5

"HELP ME turn him over," Frank said to Joe. His head reeled as he tried to comprehend what had happened. Could someone on board have poisoned Harry?

Hoping against hope that Harry might revive, Frank and Joe slipped their hands under his body and began to roll him gently onto his back. Just then there was a sharp knock on the cabin door.

"What's going on in there?" Captain Delaney's voice boomed. "Who screamed? Open this door at once!"

"Hide the markers in the closet," Frank said to Joe in a low voice. After his brother had done so, Frank unlocked the door and opened it.

A small crowd had gathered outside Harry's

door. Bob and Vic stood behind the angry captain with Dr. Wills. Frank realized that Harry's scream must have carried halfway through the ship.

"I think he's dead," Frank managed to say before the doctor rushed past him to Harry.

Frank watched him check Harry's pulse and saw that the doctor couldn't find it either. The doctor stared at Frank in shock and horror. "What happened in here?" he demanded finally.

"We were just talking," Frank said.

"Yeah," Joe added. "All of a sudden he screamed and fell to the floor. He was gone by the time we got to him."

Captain Delaney seemed unconvinced. "It's a good thing we're headed back to port," he said. "Fowler, report this to the police on the ship's phone."

As Bob ran off to do as he was told, the captain turned to Frank and Joe. "You two will stay in your cabins until the police get here," he ordered. "And I don't want this discussed with anyone until they arrive."

"But this wasn't our fault," Frank protested. "He had some kind of seizure!"

Captain Delaney shook his head. He was gray faced and obviously very worried, Frank noticed. If the captain wasn't careful, he might have a seizure of his own.

"Doctor, did you notice anything unusual

when you examined him this afternoon?" he asked.

"Nothing that might have predicted this. I'd suggested he have a full checkup on the island tomorrow."

The captain nodded gravely. Watching him, Frank realized that he actually suspected the Hardys of foul play. Frank started to protest again but realized there was no way he could convince Delaney until they had been cleared by the police.

"Doctor, you stay with the body until the authorities get here," the captain said. "Everybody else, to your cabins."

As the *Valiant* pulled up to the West End dock Frank lay on his bunk pondering the day's events and wondering who could be behind them. The trouble is, he thought, no one on the boat seemed to be a likely suspect. And why would anyone want to harm the crew in the first place? Harry Lyman hadn't been the most lovable guy, Frank admitted, but that was no reason to kill him.

To his relief, Frank heard the telltale static of a police officer's two-way radio moving down the passageway to Harry's room. "Good," he muttered, sitting up on the bunk. "Let's get this cleared up and over with."

"Frank Hardy?" Frank opened the door to confront a short, businesslike Bahamian man in the crisp uniform of a police officer. "Sergeant Mylan," he said in his English-sounding accent. "You will come with me."

"Where to?" Frank followed the sergeant to Joe's room. He felt impatient. The sooner they could explain what had happened, the sooner they'd be left alone to investigate on their own.

"We're going to the police station," the sergeant informed them as he led the way up to the main deck.

Frank froze in midstep and turned to stare at his brother. The police station? Were they really suspects, then?

"Routine questions, of course," the sergeant said. "But you may have to stay there overnight, until we receive the coroner's report."

"I don't believe this!" Joe exploded, causing the sergeant to spin instantly around, brandishing handcuffs. Seeing them, Joe backed down quickly, muttering to his older brother, "I sure hope Dad doesn't find out about this!"

It was nearly ten o'clock at night before the police were done questioning the Hardys about their involvement in Harry Lyman's death. For hours, it seemed to Frank, he and Joe had been cross-examined about what Harry had said to them before he died, how he had behaved, how well the Hardys knew him, and what they thought might really be going on on board the *Valiant*.

By the time they trudged to the cell where they had been informed they were to spend the night, Frank could barely remember his own name.

"We can't stay here," Joe protested to the sergeant one last time as he and Frank surrendered their personal belongings to the desk clerk. "We have to report to work tomorrow morning. The captain's on a tight diving schedule."

"Operations aboard the *Valiant* have been suspended pending further notification," the sergeant informed him, satisfied with himself. "The coroner's report will be in by early tomorrow morning. If it supports what you've told us, you'll be on your way soon after that."

Frank groaned, thinking of how hard this delay would be for the captain.

"Our apologies to you both for the inconvenience," the sergeant said as Frank and Joe were led away to the holding chamber.

"Right," Joe muttered under his breath. "Boy, Delaney must be steaming!"

To his surprise, Frank found that the holding tank was at least as comfortable as their cabins on board ship. "Hey, I like this," his brother said, testing the cot after they had showered.

"Very civilized," Frank agreed. But he was interrupted by an enormous yawn. "I don't know about you, but I'd better hit the sack," he said sheepishly. "Maybe this'll be straightened out by the time we wake up."

*　　*　　*

Frank was more surprised than anyone to find out that his wish had come true. He was awakened by a guard's banging on the bars of their cell.

"Sergeant wants to see you," the guard announced.

Frank and Joe followed the guard to the sergeant's office, where the little man unceremoniously handed them their bags of personal belongings.

"We have the coroner's report," he said. "Mr. Lyman died of a massive heart attack. Judging from his medical report, which we received from New York, he had a chronic heart condition that should have prevented him from diving."

"He must have kept it a secret from the captain," Joe said, still trying to wake up.

"And Dr. Wills," Frank added, frowning. It didn't make sense, he was thinking. Why would someone with a heart condition take such a dangerous chance? Could Harry Lyman's greed for gold have overpowered his common sense?

"You're free to go," the sergeant told them, standing up. "But if you don't mind, boys, I have one more question."

"Yes, sir?" Frank waited impatiently, wishing he could walk out into the bright sunshine right then and put all this behind them.

"Tell me—has either of you seen any actual treasure from the *Doña Bonita* on board?"

Frank's eyebrows shot up in surprise. Why was the sergeant so curious?

"No," Joe said. "The captain thinks they're zeroing in on something, but so far nothing valuable's turned up."

The sergeant frowned. He seemed very disappointed. "Is something wrong, sir?" Frank ventured.

The sergeant started to shake his head. Then he stopped. He moved closer to the two boys. "I shouldn't tell you this," he said in a low voice, "but perhaps later you boys will be able to help me. We have uncovered a gold artifact here on the island. One of our local criminals was foolish enough to try to sell it to an undercover customs agent. We think it may be hot, although he said it came from a sunken ship, the *Doña Bonita*. This criminal, Max Trepo, swears the artifact was given to him by one of your crew members in payment for a debt."

"Which crew member?" Joe asked.

"A Peter Duvall," the sergeant answered. "And now that man is missing, correct?"

As Frank and Joe tried to digest this new information, the sergeant added, "Apparently, this Duvall fellow is alive and active in the underworld on our island."

Frank shook his head. Gina would be glad Peter was alive, he told himself. But a criminal? He wondered how much of this was true.

"You'll keep this to yourselves, of course,"

the sergeant said, escorting the boys to the door. He shook their hands, then said in a low voice, "We understand you have some experience in the area of detection. If you find anything suspicious on board ship, I trust you'll let us know."

"Of course, Sergeant," Frank said, covering his surprise. But Joe wasn't even listening because he'd spotted Gina waiting for them in the parking lot and was waving to get her attention.

Frank said goodbye to the little sergeant, then followed his brother to Gina's dusty hatchback.

"Is everything all right?" Gina asked as the brothers got in and slammed the doors.

"You bet!" said Joe. "Boy, is it great to be sprung! Thanks for picking us up, Gina."

"No problem," she said. "Any news?"

"Yeah!" Joe said eagerly. Then he remembered that it wouldn't be good news for Gina, and his face fell.

Gina's hands tightened on the steering wheel as she turned out of the police station lot. "Go ahead," she said grimly. "But this time I'll keep my eyes on the road."

When Joe and Frank had told Gina the story, the marine archaeologist was stunned. "Listen, I know my brother," she said angrily. "He wouldn't steal anything. And if he was okay, he'd write to me."

"Did your brother ever mention the name Max Trepo in his letters?" Frank asked.

"No. He practically never left the ship, as far as I could tell," she answered.

The three of them mulled this fact over for a moment. Then Frank noticed that they were headed away from the dock. "Where are you taking us?" he asked Gina.

Gina became embarrassed. "Well, you know operations on the ship were suspended, don't you?" she said.

"Yeah," said Joe. "The captain must be hopping mad."

Gina nodded. "He's in court trying to reverse the decision right now. Meanwhile, I wanted to check something out. I overheard Vic and Alastair talking this morning. I heard them say something about Peter and an island hotel called the Easy Life."

"So you want us to pay it a visit," said Joe.

Gina nodded. "It's in a bad part of town. I figured I'd better take you guys along."

Frank glanced out the window and saw that they were passing the airport, headed north on the island. Soon, the grand hotels and golf courses on the south shore had faded into rows of smaller buildings and, finally, dilapidated shacks. It was in this area that he finally spotted the blistered sign that read, Easy Life Hotel, and underneath that, Daily Rates.

"There it is," Joe said to Gina.

She parked the car next to several other cars on the parched grass in front of the building.

Just as the three of them reached the door, it burst open, knocking Gina back into Joe's arms.

Before Frank could react, two men in dirty sweatshirts and jeans raced down the rickety stairs. All that registered in Frank's mind were a tattoo on one man's forearm and an earring hanging from the earlobe of the other.

Joe helped Gina up and then he and his brother took off after the two men, who were running toward a clump of trees that surrounded the hotel property. Just as they reached the first trees, Joe grabbed one of the guys around the ankles, bringing him to the ground.

Meanwhile, Frank collared the second one, twisting his arm and sending him to his knees.

"You little—" Joe's captive started to get up. His muscles rippled as he grabbed Joe around the neck. Frank moved to help his brother, but his own captive spun around and started to resist.

Frank almost didn't hear Gina's shout from the front steps.

"Frank!" she screamed. "Watch out behind you!"

Frank whirled around to see an enormous man lumbering across the lawn toward them.

The stranger had a baseball bat. He was racing straight for Frank.

Chapter

6

"NOW WHAT?" Joe had to make up his mind fast. Should he let go of the squirming guy he had pinned to the ground and go after the monster who was moving in on his brother? Or should he keep a grip on at least one of these goons? Taking a chance, he let go of his opponent. Instinct told him to go after the bat first.

As he ran toward the screaming man with the baseball bat, he saw that Frank had let go of his captive, too. But to Joe's surprise, the first two thugs instantly got to their feet and took off into the woods.

"Hoodlums!" the giant yelled after the fugitives, racing past the Hardys and waving his bat. "Deadbeats! Don't show up again! I know who you are! I'm warning you!"

"What's going on?" Joe said, stunned. "You're not after us?"

The man gave up chasing the others and stopped in his tracks, dropping the bat heavily on the grass. Then he turned to Joe. "Chasing you?" he said in a cheerful voice. "Why should I? I don't even know you."

Bewildered, Joe and Frank followed him back to the front steps, where Gina sat nursing a scraped elbow. "What was that all about?" she asked.

"Oh, just a couple of deadbeats trying to run out on their bill," the giant said in his mild local accent. "Happens all the time here. It's getting so I look forward to a good chase to liven up my day."

Joe shook his head. The enormous man's stomach, which hung over his belt by a hefty margin, heaved up and down as he gasped for breath. "Thanks for your help," the man said. "My name's Manfred, by the way." He held out a sweaty palm.

"I'm Joe Hardy." Joe shook the hand. "This is my brother Frank, and Gina Duv—uh, Daniels." The man must weigh at least three hundred and fifty pounds, Joe guessed. With that much weight on him it was hard to tell his age, but Joe figured he must be around thirty.

"Why don't you all come inside and have a cool drink?" Manfred suggested, smiling.

"There's a soda machine in the lobby. Did you plan on staying here?"

"Not really," Joe said as he followed Gina and Frank into the tiny front room. Inside he saw only a small counter and a soda machine. Manfred had already retrieved four cans and was popping one open for each of them.

Joe accepted a soda from Manfred's massive hand. "Actually, we were wondering if you could give us some information," he said, wiping the sweat from his forehead with the sleeve of his T-shirt.

"Information?" Manfred's open face turned suddenly suspicious.

"Yeah," Frank said. "We're looking for a friend of ours. We heard he might have stayed here a couple of weeks ago. Maybe you remember him."

Manfred's smile split his face in two. "Well now, that's a different story. I wouldn't have been so free with the sodas if I'd known you weren't paying customers." He rubbed the back of his head.

"Okay," Frank said, pulling out his wallet and handing Manfred a twenty. "Let us have a peek at your ledger to find out if he stayed here or not?"

Manfred nodded, still smiling. He pocketed the twenty and turned the ledger around so that it faced the trio. "This much for twenty dollars," he said, "but anything else is extra."

Joe peered over Frank's shoulder as he flipped back through the pages. "There it is!" Gina said suddenly, pointing to an entry halfway down a page.

Joe saw it in the same instant. The entry was dated Monday, July 31. The name was Peter Duvall.

Frank flipped back several more pages. "He was registered here for three days," he said. "July thirty-first through August second."

"And he disappeared on the thirtieth," Gina said softly. "But wait a minute. That's not his handwriting."

"Of course not." Manfred's voice boomed in the small room, startling them. "It's my handwriting! It don't do me no good to have people sign in if I can't read their names!"

Joe peered at the ledger again. Sure enough, all the entries were scrawled in the same messy hand. "Do you remember Peter Duvall?" he asked the hotel keeper.

"What do you want to know about him? He's *your* friend, isn't he?" Manfred's eyes narrowed slightly. "Besides, I told you. Twenty dollars covers the ledger only. Anything else is extra."

With a sigh, Frank took out another twenty and held it out to their host. But as Manfred started to snatch it, Frank pulled it back. "*After* you give us the information," he said. "I want to make sure it's worth it."

Manfred grinned amiably and shook his head.

"I don't know what you nice young people want with that Duvall person, anyway," he said. "He's as bad as the two who took off out of here a few minutes ago. If I remember right, he was about your age," he said, eyeing Joe critically. "A mite shorter, no beard, and dark, curly hair. Didn't bring any luggage with him. Wore the same clothes for three days. I remember that much."

Joe glanced at Gina, who nodded. Apparently, Manfred's description added up.

"Did anyone visit him here?" Joe asked.

Manfred snorted. "People don't meet here. They sleep and then leave. His kind would've met folks at Waves."

"What's Waves?" Frank asked.

"A disco out by the airport. Now, is there anything else I can do for you?"

Joe noticed his eyes resting on the twenty. "Okay," he said, taking it from Frank and handing it to Manfred. "Thanks for your help."

"Hey, one good turn deserves another." Manfred smiled and stuffed the bill into his pocket.

As Joe, Gina, and Frank started across the dry lawn toward their car, Joe noticed a bit of paper fluttering on the hatchback's windshield. "What's that?" he asked, moving faster. Had the thugs they'd chased left a threatening message on their car?

"Probably an advertisement," Frank remarked. But as Joe pulled the tiny slip of paper out from under the windshield wiper his expression showed it was no advertisement.

" 'Keep out of this,' " he read aloud to Frank and Gina. " 'Believe me, you won't be able to handle it.' "

"Those jerks we chased must have written it," he decided. "What cowards, slipping a note on our car instead of confronting us."

"Let me see it," Gina said, taking the paper from him.

As she read the note, she turned suddenly pale and had to lean against the car for support.

"What is it?" Frank asked.

Gina's eyes were round. "Remember my telling you that Peter used to write to me every week?" she said.

Joe stared at her. He knew exactly what she meant.

The threatening note had to be in Peter's handwriting!

Chapter

7

"IT'S FROM YOUR BROTHER, isn't it?" Joe asked Gina, taking back the note.

She nodded.

"It's okay," she said, taking a deep breath. "At least he's still alive. Do you mind driving, Frank? I don't think I'm up to it."

After they'd climbed into the car, Frank said, "Let's stop somewhere to eat, and after that I think we need to get back to the ship. I want to talk to the crew, and especially to Poison."

"I don't understand how Peter could have changed this much," Gina said in a low voice. "He never did anything bad before."

"Don't worry about it yet, Gina," Joe advised her. "You don't know what he's doing. There's a lot to clear up here."

Frank glanced at his brother. That was the understatement of the week, he thought. Here they were, saddled with an invisible crew member who wrote threatening notes, a captain whose chances for wealth were dwindling before his eyes, one dead diver, and a group of bewildered kids who probably wondered how they were going to afford a plane ticket home. Right now nothing—and no one—connected with this expedition made any sense.

It was growing dark by the time Frank pulled the car into the marina's lot. He led the way up the *Valiant*'s gangplank.

"No one's here," he said as the three of them surveyed the deck.

"Let's check out the lounge." Gina led the way to the companionway.

Frank could see why the crew hung out in the dining room on their hours off. He entered to see Vic and Bob slouched comfortably at the big table, playing cards. A huge bowl of potato chips sat half empty between them. Alastair sat sideways in an armchair in a corner, reading a magazine and listening to Caribbean music on the radio.

If there hadn't been a death on board the day before, Frank reflected, the crew would probably have enjoyed the extra time off.

"Hey, guys, join the game!" Bob spread his

cards on the table. "The captain's off trying to get the diving ban lifted, so we working folks are taking the evening off. You play gin rummy?"

"Sure," said Joe, joining him. "Bet I can slaughter you, too."

"We'll see about that." Bob shuffled the cards as Vic watched, chewing thoughtfully on a toothpick. Gina got a soda from the kitchen and sat down at the table, while Frank joined Alastair by the magazines. Frank glanced at Alastair's hand as he settled down into one of the easy chairs. His eyes widened. Peter Duvall's ring was gone.

"Lose your ring?" he asked as the group at the table started playing a raucous game of gin rummy.

Alastair lifted his head. "Huh? Oh." He smiled nervously. "I thought with everything that's going on, I'd put it in a safe place. If you know what I mean."

Frank nodded. He didn't know what Alastair meant, but he didn't want to press him right then. It was hard to imagine that someone as easygoing as Alastair was up to no good, but the fact that he had Peter's ring was suspicious.

Frank noticed Jason standing in the doorway, his hands shoved deep in his pockets.

"Looks like we're all accounted for," the Southerner said to no one in particular. He locked gazes with Frank. "How'd it go at the police station? You guys get arrested or what?"

Frank stifled his annoyance. "They let us go after they got the coroner's report. Harry died of a heart attack."

Alastair tossed his magazine back on the bookshelf and stood up. "Excuse me," he said, squeezing past Jason. "I think I'll turn in for the night."

Frank watched him go, then met Joe's gaze for an instant. He could tell Joe wondered the same thing he did. Was there some kind of hostility between Jason and Alastair, or was the ex-cook just feeling uneasy?

"Don't mind Poison," Bob said as though reading their minds. "He gets moody sometimes. That's another reason we'd just as soon fix our own food around here."

A moment later the heavy tread of the captain sounded in the passageway. His leonine head poked through the doorway. "Evening, all," he said gruffly. Frank noticed that Delaney wore khaki trousers and a neatly pressed short-sleeved shirt. It was the first time he'd seen the captain with a shirt on.

"The ban's lifted," the captain announced. "We dive as scheduled tomorrow. Vic and Gina will be our first team, and Frank and Jason will pair up in the afternoon. If I were you, I'd rest up. Deck call is seven o'clock sharp."

He disappeared as abruptly as he'd arrived.

"Well, that was fun," Bob said, folding his cards and tossing them into the middle of the table. "Glad it's not me going down tomorrow, hey, Joe?"

"I don't know," Joe observed, stacking his cards facedown on top of Bob's. "Sometimes it feels safer down there."

By the next afternoon Frank had begun to wonder if the entire crew of the *Valiant* wished they were safely at the bottom of the Caribbean. Gina and Vic's morning dive had been uneventful. And as the hours passed and the summer sun beat down on the rocking ship, Delaney grew increasingly angry.

"Why aren't you suited up yet?" he growled at Frank as the crew prepared to move some distance to the west. Frank had heard from Vic that Delaney had been studying his charts again and had decided to try a new location.

Frank didn't bother to answer. By the time the *Valiant* had anchored some distance from the island, he had his diving gear strapped on and checked. By then it was almost two o'clock, and the afternoon sun was making him sweat as he waited on the deck. All around him, waves rolled toward the little ship, causing it to toss its occupants back and forth a little.

"Take the markers," the captain ordered gruffly, shoving them into Frank's hands.

"Dumb amateurs. Do I have to remind you about every single thing?"

Ignoring his insults, Frank discreetly weighed the markers in each hand and decided they weighed the same. He hooked them to his belt, then backed up the rail with Jason. Frank had the Air Lift while Jason clutched the magnetometer.

"Ready, partner?" Frank said to the shy teenager. To his surprise, Jason scowled. He seemed furious about something. What now? Frank wondered impatiently. If I didn't know better, I'd think there was a curse on the entire crew!

The splash into the cool ocean water came as a great relief. And so, Frank thought as he sank slowly beneath the surface, did the silence.

The water in that area of the ocean was deep blue. Frank hadn't gone down far before he had to turn his head lamp on. There were fewer brightly colored fish as well, but Frank and Jason's lights illuminated darker, larger species that moved slowly through their own silent kingdom.

Wow! I wonder if Delaney knows about this? Frank thought, aiming his head lamp down toward where the ocean floor should have been. The bottom fell off sharply into a deep, black chasm.

Frank looked at Jason. The chasm seemed bottomless. If the *Doña Bonita* sank there, he thought, Delaney could say goodbye to the gold.

As Jason started off on an exploration of the floor near the edge of the chasm, Frank hung back. Jason's attitude bothered him, and he thought it might be a better idea to separate for a while. He began moving slowly in the opposite direction, also following the chasm's edge. He found it hard to see in the dark water, and shapes in the sand were often misleading.

Suddenly Frank spotted something unusual in the water. He swam a foot or two lower, peering through his mask.

Something white was sticking out from beneath an outcropping of rock. Frank reached down and pulled on it. It came loose easily. Frank realized it was one of the *Valiant*'s white markers!

But that's impossible, Frank told himself. They've never dived here before.

Glancing over his shoulder, Frank took out one of the markers the captain had given him and weighed it against the new one. Even underwater he could tell the new marker was heavier. He placed the captain's marker where the heavier one had been and hung the heavy marker from his belt.

Just then he noticed Jason, a good distance away, waving the magnetometer in the water to get his attention. Frank swam over to join him. He watched Jason signal his impatience to get to work, nodded to show he understood, and began following him with the Air Lift vacuum.

It was frustrating to follow Jason in the direction opposite from where he had found the mysterious marker, but Frank didn't know whether he could trust Jason. At least now, after twenty minutes of fruitless searching, the magnetometer started beeping.

Jason brought the detector closer to two encrusted objects that lay side by side, half-buried in the sand at the very edge of the chasm. They were small, Frank noticed, but their identical size and shape made him hope they were something worthwhile.

Excited, Frank dug the objects out of the sand. He held them up for Jason to see. But as Jason swam closer, he knocked Frank's hand. The objects went sailing. Frank managed to catch one of them, but the other fell into the blackness of the chasm.

Frank tried to stifle his disappointment as he watched the mysterious object disappear. That might have been a museum piece, he realized.

He looked over to see Jason miming an apology by smacking his head with his hand. Frank shook his head, dropped the remaining relic into his net bag, and signaled that it was time to surface. He didn't want to take any chances with what they still had.

Up top, Frank could feel the suspense as the captain and crew waited anxiously for the divers to board.

"I think we found something," he said as soon as he could catch his breath. He took the relic out of his bag and held it up for the others to see. Jason stood to the side, scowling. Frank guessed he wished he'd been the hero for the day.

"Is that it?" The captain grabbed the piece from Frank's hand.

"That's all," Frank said. Jason didn't contradict him. Neither diver wanted to frustrate Delaney more by telling him what they'd lost.

The crew crowded around the captain to get a peek at the object, which seemed to be roughly in the shape of a cross. Frank watched Dr. Wills and Alastair gazing at the barnacle-covered mound with skeptical frowns.

"Looks interesting," the doctor said noncommittally. "Of course, it could turn out to be worthless junk."

"Let's hope not," the captain said, sounding more optimistic than before. "Poison, pack this into a plastic case. We'll run it down to the lab tomorrow night, the minute we hit shore."

"Aye-aye, sir," the crew member agreed.

Frank backed away and moved to where Joe and Gina were standing at the edge of the crowd. "Come with me," he murmured in a low voice. "I have something to show you."

He led the pair downstairs to his cabin, where he locked his door behind them, took off the rest of his gear, and threw on a terry cloth robe. Then he rummaged through his suitcase until he brought out a black plastic box.

"Remember this?" He held the box up for Joe's inspection. "You wanted to leave it at the airport, right?"

"It hasn't come in handy so far," Joe said defensively.

"It will now," Frank responded. "This is a sonar gauge," he explained to Gina. "It gives accurate depth readings using sonar, but it can also detect the presence of sonar in any area. By pushing this button, I can activate or turn off any sonar signal within its range."

"I know what it is," Gina said impatiently. "What about it?"

Frank turned on the portable radio on his writing desk, filling the cabin with sound. Then he retrieved the heavy white marker from his gear, set it next to the radio, and aimed the black box at it. Dramatically, he pushed the red button on its side.

Immediately the marker began beeping.

Joe and Gina stared at the marker.

"That's a sonar?" Gina asked as Frank turned off the depth gauge.

"You said it," Frank answered, relieved. He had suspected this when he had first found the marker, but now he was sure.

Someone aboard ship was secretly marking the real treasure site for himself!

Chapter

8

"THIS MEANS that someone's using these markers to stake out the treasure site."

"But why would anyone do that?" Joe stared at his brother, uncomprehending.

"I'm not sure yet," Frank admitted as he replaced the black box and carefully hid the marker in the closet. Joe watched him, making a mental note that they'd have to replace the sonar on tomorrow's dive, before whoever had placed it was alerted.

"Maybe Captain Delaney doesn't want to share with the crew after all," Gina suggested. "Maybe he intends to come back alone later and rake in the gold."

"Maybe," Frank agreed. "But he's the one who brought us out here today. Why would he lead us straight to the treasure if he meant to hide it?"

Joe shook his head. "You're right, but we're definitely getting closer. And I have a feeling this is going to link up with Peter in a way we haven't figured yet."

He glanced at Gina. She looked suddenly sad, and he was sorry he'd mentioned her brother. "I'm going to get something to eat and turn in early," she said, standing. "You guys want to join me in the galley?"

"Best idea I've heard all day." Joe followed her to the door. He wished he could be more help to Gina. Maybe after a hamburger his investigative talents would kick in.

The policy in the dining room was still self-serve, so Joe volunteered to throw together deluxe hamburgers for all three of them. "Served with chips on the side," he announced, sliding a paper plate heaped with food in front of Gina at the big table. Frank's hamburger was even bigger. "Fresh tomatoes bought on the island this morning. Mustard imported from southern France."

"*Merci*, Chef Joseph," Gina teased, digging into her burger. "All that's missing is a little violin music."

"I'd play for you," Joe said, setting his own plate on the table and pulling out a chair, "but the smell of beef has drowned out my artistic sensibilities."

As he sat down, Joe saw Alastair pause in the doorway. The instant he saw the three teenagers, he started to retreat.

"Hey, hold on, buddy," Joe said. "We won't bite. Come on in and I'll put together some leftovers."

"That's okay." Alastair hovered on the threshold. "I didn't know anyone was here. I think I'll eat in my room."

"Come on in," Frank said, getting up and walking over to Alastair. "I wanted to ask you something, anyway."

"Like what?" he asked suspiciously.

"I was wondering. You're from the Bahamas." Frank smiled. "We were driving around the north shore yesterday. I thought maybe you knew that area."

Alastair's eyes widened. "You were on the north shore? That's where I grew up."

"Oh, yeah?" Joe swallowed a mouthful of hamburger. "You ever hear of the Easy Life?"

"What do you think I'm living, man?" Alastair laughed weakly, but Joe could see he didn't like being cross-examined.

"No, it's a hotel," Joe said casually. "Run by a guy named Manfred?"

Alastair shook his head, backing toward the corridor again. "Don't know him," he said. "I haven't been back there in a while."

"How come I heard you mention the place

to Vic yesterday, then?" Gina asked in a harsh voice.

Alastair stared at her in silence. As footsteps approached from the stairs, he said, "You must have overheard someone else. I'll see you later."

He escaped out the door just as Vic sauntered in, saying, "Did I hear you guys talking about me in here?"

The Hardys and Gina regarded him in silence. Vic appeared to be innocent enough, Joe reflected. But nobody was innocent on this ship. At least not until they'd proved it.

"We were talking about the Easy Life Hotel," Frank said. "You know the place?"

Vic laughed, heading for the kitchen. "Man, I don't know any place on this island. Delaney works us so hard I barely get off this ship. And on my days off, Bob keeps me busy with his card games."

"You were talking about the Easy Life and Peter Duvall with Poison yesterday," Gina insisted. "I know, because I heard you."

"Hey, what is this?" Vic returned to the table with a bag of pretzels and a soda. "All I'm trying to do is fill my stomach and I get the third degree."

Joe watched him eat. Vic sure didn't act like a guilty man, he admitted. He could put food away almost as fast as Joe himself. Gina was also watching Vic.

She must be worried sick about her brother

by now, Joe thought. He exchanged glances with Frank, who nodded. Joe knew he was thinking the same thing.

"Restaurant's closed," he said lightly, standing up and clearing their plates from the table. "Time for a good night's sleep. I bet we'll feel better tomorrow."

To Joe's disappointment, both the morning and afternoon dives proved fruitless. Since neither the Hardys nor Gina was chosen to go under, they were unable to replace the sonar-equipped marker. That night the ship docked to let Dr. Wills take the single artifact to the lab for analysis, and the next day the captain tried a new location.

By Saturday, Joe began to fear for the captain's sanity. He had only one week left to find the treasure, and Joe had a good idea by now how expensive this operation must be.

"If I were Delaney, I'd look for an easy job on a cruise line," he confided to Gina as the *Valiant* chugged into port on Saturday night. They were sitting on folding chairs on deck, looking at the full moon hanging low over the Caribbean. It would have been a perfect evening, Joe reflected, if the fate of the captain and of Peter Duvall wasn't hanging over their heads.

Joe heard footsteps approaching. He twisted in his chair and saw Frank walking toward them. His brother seemed upset about something.

"What's up?" Joe asked, resting his feet on the railing.

"I'm worried about the marker," Frank said in a low voice, squatting on the deck next to the other two. "We've got to find a way to replace it before someone notices it's gone."

"Maybe we'll go back there next week," Gina said. "If the artifact turns out to be real—and the captain's on the up and up—we'll probably spend the rest of the trip there."

"We can't take that chance," Frank said.

"We could rent a boat tomorrow, on our day off," suggested Joe. "Ride out and replace the marker while everyone else is docked."

That reminded Joe of something. "I've been thinking about what Harry was trying to tell us right before he died. Do you think it could have something to do with those markers?"

Frank started to answer, but a voice interrupted from behind, startling the three of them. "Hey, Frank, you have a minute?" Vic asked as he sauntered over toward them.

"Sure, Vic," Frank said, turning guiltily. "We were just making plans for tomorrow."

"That's what I wanted to ask you," Vic said, moving his toothpick from one side of his mouth to the other. "Bob and I are going to the motorboat races tomorrow afternoon. You guys want to come?"

"We're, uh, tied up during the day." Joe motioned to Gina to keep quiet. He knew Gina was suspicious of Vic because he hadn't admitted knowing anything about the Easy Life. He worried that she might give away their hand if she confronted him again.

"And we're going to a disco tonight," Gina added, despite Joe's glance. "You ever hear of Waves?"

Vic was surprised. "Poison told me about that place. It's supposed to be pretty wild."

"Good," Gina said shortly. "We need to unwind."

As soon as the ship docked, Joe, Gina, and Frank hurried to Gina's car. Wild or not, Joe was looking forward to going to the disco. He knew he'd feel better after he'd danced off some of his pent-up energy.

"I hope you don't mind stopping by my apartment first," Gina said as she drove. "I've got to change out of these cut-offs. I don't want to embarrass you guys in your nice clean shirts."

Joe laughed. "No problem. It'll be interesting to see what a marine archaeologist's apartment looks like."

"If you're expecting china and lace, forget it," Gina said lightly. "I just rented this place two weeks ago. It's a dumping ground for my bare necessities, and that's it."

Half an hour later Joe saw that Gina had been telling the truth. He and Frank checked out her small efficiency while waiting for her to shower and change. It was nearly bare but spotlessly clean. On the table next to the daybed was a framed photograph of Gina with a middle-aged woman and an older, gray-haired man. Joe read the inscription aloud: " 'To our brilliant daughter. Love, Mom and William.' "

"What are you guys standing around for?"

Joe turned to see Gina posing in the door of the bathroom. She'd changed into a short black dress, heels, and dark stockings. Long gold earrings dangled against her sun-bleached hair. "Do I pass muster?" she demanded, turning around for the boys' inspection.

"Hey, straight A's in my book," Joe said with a grin. "Let's dance!"

It took a moment for Frank's eyes and ears to adjust to the scene as the trio entered through the disco's wide double doors. The music was cranked up so high that Frank could feel the bass riffs vibrate under his feet, and the flashing, colored light show nearly blinded him.

"All right!" he heard his brother say as Joe led Gina toward the transparent dance floor. Glowing red and green neon lights turned the dancers colors as they moved.

"I can tell you this wouldn't be Peter's scene," Gina protested, following Joe.

"Don't worry about it," Frank called after her. "You guys have fun. I'll see what I can find out."

Frank moved around the edge of the club, checking out the clientele. Waves seemed to be a hangout for the island's rougher types. Regulars in black leather and studs called to one another across the crowded room. A few tourists were crowded in near the door. A sullen-looking, heavyset bouncer lounged against the wall near the entryway. Frank saw that he wore a name tag reading Gus. Frank remembered what the police chief had told him about Peter Duvall's involvement with the criminal Max Trepo. Perhaps Max would hang out in a place like this.

"Hey, Gus!" Frank approached the bouncer as though they were old friends. "I can't find Max Trepo tonight. You seen him?"

The bouncer eyed Frank through narrowed eyes. "You blind?" he yelled above the music. "He's right behind you."

Frank turned to where Gus pointed. A skinny man was sitting alone at a table near the dance floor. In a second two toughs walked over and huddled with him.

As Frank approached the table, he watched one of the men nudge Max's arm, alerting him to Frank's presence. Max looked up as Frank stood before him.

"Something I can do for you?" Max drawled. Frank flinched. Max's voice sounded as if it were being filtered through gravel.

Frank decided to take a chance. "Peter Duvall said I'd find you here," he shouted.

Just as he opened his mouth to speak, the band stopped playing. Frank's words carried across the entire club.

"What?" Max pushed back his chair as though Frank had slapped him and stood up with clenched fists. He shot a look at his cohorts, and before Frank knew what was happening, they lunged toward him.

"Wait!" Frank took a step back, looking around wildly. He caught a glimpse of Joe running to him just as one of Max's thugs grabbed him in a hammerlock.

"Hey, what's going—" Frank started to yell, but was interrupted as the second guy punched him in the stomach.

Frank's head dangled from his neck. The floor reeled before his eyes.

I've got to fight back, he told himself.

He lifted his gaze to try again, and found himself eye to eye with Max's six-inch stiletto!

Chapter

9

"OH, NO, you don't!" Joe jumped over Max Trepo's table and knocked the skinny crook forward into one of his own men.

"Aaaugh!" The bodyguard screamed as Max's stiletto plunged into his arm. Reflexively, he threw his boss backward. Max Trepo landed on his spine on a table five feet away.

Joe released his brother from the grip of Trepo's other, stunned bodyguard and sent a flying karate kick to the guard's stomach. He realized that the entire club was in an uproar now. The man whose table Max had landed on smashed a pitcher on the crook's head.

"Not bad, Joe," Frank muttered, keeping an eye on the bodyguard who sat nursing his knife wound nearby.

Joe nodded, waiting to catch his breath. The trio didn't seem much of a threat anymore. The two bodyguards were on the floor, and Max sat moaning at a table as a waitress put ice on the knot on his head.

"Who's that guy?" Joe asked his brother.

"Max Trepo. The crook the sergeant told us about. I mentioned Peter's name, and he blew up."

Gina retrieved the stiletto from under the table. "Uh-oh," she said, glancing over Joe's shoulder. "Here comes trouble."

Joe turned to see the bouncer approaching them, red-faced. "Okay, everybody, into the back room," he demanded, signaling the band to start playing again. He glared at Frank. "I knew you were trouble the minute I saw you. Now you're going to have to deal with me."

Gus ushered the Hardys, Gina, and Max into an office crammed full of cardboard boxes piled nearly to the ceiling.

"Max, one more stunt like this and you're barred for good," Gus fumed as the five of them crowded in. "We're not going to get shut down again because of you."

"They went after me first, I swear," the skinny man said angrily. "I just defended myself."

"All I said was that Peter Duvall sent me," Frank retorted.

"Yeah, that's all," Max said sulkily. "It just so happens I talked to Peter tonight. And he told me some guys were going to come after me. That's why I was on the lookout for you."

"Peter called you tonight?" Gina asked.

"Ain't that what I said, lady?"

"When was the last time you saw him?" Joe demanded.

Max eyed him suspiciously. "What business is it of yours?"

"All right, all right, that's enough," Gus said. "All I need's another fight in here. You folks get out of here. And I don't want any more trouble. Is that clear?"

This time Gus ushered them out the club's back exit. Joe watched Max readjust his sports jacket in an effort to regain his dignity. Then Max led the way out of the alley, toward a black car with tinted windows where they could see his bodyguards waiting.

"Wait, Mr. Trepo," Gina called after him. Before Joe could stop her, she had caught him by the arm.

"Yeah?" he growled, slowing only slightly.

"Please." Gina tried to make eye contact with Trepo, but he wouldn't look at her. "I wanted to give this back to you." She held out the stiletto.

Joe gasped and started to go after her, but Frank held him back. Slowly the brothers approached the pair, careful not to make Max or his guards nervous.

"Can't you tell me where Peter is?" Joe heard Gina plead.

Max shook his head in annoyance. "I never should've listened to that guy," he muttered. "He's the one who got me messed up with the cops."

"I know," Joe ventured, stepping forward to join them. "He tried to pull the same trick on us. You're talking about those antique things he gave us, right?"

To Joe, it seemed as if Max's ears literally pricked up. "Yeah. The gold?" he said roughly. "Turns out he might have stolen it, you know."

"We found out the hard way." Frank played along with Joe. "Did he tell you where he got the stuff? I'm gonna punch whoever started this."

"He gave me some story about it coming from some sunken ship," Max drawled, warming up a little. "I never believed him, but he told me there was plenty more where that came from. He had to have smuggled it."

"He got a grand up front from us," Gina said.

"He told us the gold was worth five times that much," Max said. "That was over a week ago. He never delivered. We ain't heard from him since."

Joe glanced at Trepo and saw that he was buying their story. "We ought to brain him," Joe said, trying to sound tough. "Tell me where to find him, Max. Let me do us both a favor."

Max brightened for a moment, then shrugged. "I wait for him to call me here." He indicated the club. "Most of our deals are done by phone. And he always does the calling."

"You expecting another call soon?" Frank asked.

Max frowned. "He promised he'd call me here again tomorrow. But I can't hold my breath."

Joe snapped his fingers. "I have an idea. If he calls, you set up a meeting with him here for tomorrow night. We'll show up, too, and give him the third degree."

A slow grin appeared on Max's face. "I've got a better idea," he said. "I know a guy who'll fly in from Miami. He's got some funny ideas about how to handle double-crossers. You guys chip in, and he'll take Peter out for good."

Out of the corner of his eye, Joe saw Gina stiffen. He tried to move between her and Max, but it was too late.

"No!" she cried out, stepping toward the crook.

"Huh?" Max turned to her.

"What she means is," Joe said, shouldering aside Gina, who looked livid, "what good would it do to get rid of him? He owes us money, and since the cops confiscated your gold, he still owes you money, too."

"Yeah, but I got my reputation to worry about," Max insisted.

"So do we," Joe said. "But we want our

money. Leave Peter to us. We'll take care of him. Agreed?"

Joe heard the black car's engine rev at the end of the alley. One of the bodyguards had gotten out and was moving toward them.

Max straightened his shoulders and moved forward. "See you tomorrow," he muttered to Joe.

"Count on it," Joe called after him.

The three young people watched Max climb into his car. The headlights snapped on, casting long shadows into the alley.

Just before the car door closed, Max Trepo leaned out and stared back at Joe. "Like I said earlier," he called to him, "I'm giving my friend in Miami a call. Just in case you can't talk sense into Duvall on your own."

Joe squeezed Gina's arm before she could go after the crook. "Good idea," he called loudly.

"Oh, and one other thing." Max's voice sounded threatening. "My friend, the one in Miami, better think you three are on the level, too. I'd hate to think of what would happen to you if he didn't."

The door closed, and the car screeched away into the blackness.

Chapter

10

"I DON'T BELIEVE THIS!" Gina leaned back against the wall as the sound of the car's engine faded in the distance. "My brother, a smuggler! It doesn't make sense!"

"There could be other explanations," Frank assured her. At the moment he couldn't think of any because the loud beat of the club's music prevented him from thinking clearly. Great, he said to himself. Now we get to deal with a Bahamian hood, a hit man from Miami, and whoever else is behind all this.

He followed Joe and Gina to her car, searching for a way out of this mess.

"If either of you had ever met Peter, you'd realize he couldn't have anything to do with this," Gina insisted, unlocking the car door.

"There's got to be some explanation for that note in his handwriting on my windshield. Peter wouldn't have written that, he'd have warned me in person!"

"There's no use talking about this now," Frank decided. "We're too tired to come up with any answers."

As they turned onto the main road, he changed the subject and decided to give Gina something to do, something to think about besides Peter. "Do you think you could rent a boat for us tomorrow so we can replace the marker I took?"

"Sure." Drops of water splashed the windshield as it started to rain.

"And one more thing." Frank caught her eye in the rearview mirror after she switched on the windshield wipers. "I was wondering if you could show us a picture of Peter. We've been searching for him, and we don't even know what he looks like."

Gina blinked, startled. "Of course," she said. "We'll stop by my apartment."

By the time they reached Gina's street a river of water was rushing beside the curbstones. "This is some thunderstorm," Frank remarked as the three of them prepared to make a run for it.

"It happens a lot," Gina told him. "Summer's the rainy season. When we get inside, I'll make some tea."

They splashed across the road to Gina's building, laughing in spite of themselves. When they reached Gina's upstairs apartment, she passed out towels and went into the kitchen to heat up the kettle.

"The photos are in the top dresser drawer," she called over her shoulder. "Help yourselves."

Frank opened the drawer and found an assortment of photographs and press clippings lying inside. Frank realized with a jolt that Gina had probably brought them along to use in missing-person posters or to show to the police.

"He looks like a nice guy," Joe remarked as they flipped through photographs showing Peter holding a swimming trophy, graduating from high school, and wearing scuba gear. Peter was just as Frank had heard him described: dark-haired, beardless, of medium height. Except for his intelligent, brown-eyed gaze, he could be one of a million other guys.

"Look at this," said Joe, picking up one of the clippings. Frank read silently along with him. The article, from the local paper, told of the *Valiant*'s search for sunken treasure, and discussed the possibility that any findings should belong to the Bahamas.

"I bet that had Delaney up in arms for weeks," Frank remarked as Gina entered with the tea cups on a wooden tray.

"This is my favorite," she said, pointing to one of the photos. She lifted out another one of the clippings that included a picture of the entire *Valiant* crew. "This was taken on their first day aboard," she said. "Peter mailed it to me."

Frank took the clipping and examined the picture closely. The captain and Dr. Wills stood in the center, with Jason, Harry, Peter, Vic, Bob, and Alastair huddled around them.

"They all look so happy," Joe commented, peering over Frank's shoulder.

Frank nodded slowly. He wished he could have been a crew member before all the trouble had started.

"One diver dead," he murmured, picking up his cup of tea. "One missing. And a very suspicious underwater marker. I do wonder what's really going on."

"I think Poison is hiding something," Gina confessed after she'd passed a cup to Joe and took one for herself. "For one thing, he has my brother's ring. For another, he flat-out lied to us about the Easy Life Hotel."

"Well, we've been acting weird lately," Joe pointed out. "We keep asking funny questions— maybe he thinks *we're* responsible for what's been going on."

Gina shrugged her shoulders. "Maybe we'll get to the bottom of this tomorrow night, when my brother is supposed to show up at Waves," she said. "Meanwhile, I'll rent a boat tomorrow morning and pick you both up at the ship."

"Great," said Frank, setting his teacup down

on the tray and standing up to go. "And stop worrying about Peter, Gina. We'll get our hands on him tomorrow, or else."

The rain had stopped by the time they all left Gina's apartment to get in her car. They skirted enormous puddles in the street. Halfway across, Gina stopped and clutched at Joe's arm.

"What's wrong?" Frank followed Gina's gaze, trying to see what had startled her.

"Behind that hedge—I thought I saw something move," she whispered.

Frank tensed. "Get in the back seat of the car," he ordered. "Lock the doors and put the keys in the ignition. We'll be right there."

This time Gina did as instructed. As soon as she was safely in the car, Frank and Joe sprinted toward the hedge she'd indicated. It was deserted, but Frank did see a shape running close to the curb halfway down the block.

He moved closer, with Joe right on his heels, and saw the figure climb onto a motorbike.

Joe started to run past his brother, but Frank reached out to stop him. "We'll make better time with the car," he whispered. Joe nodded, and the two of them raced back to the hatchback.

Gina had seen them coming and unlocked the doors. Joe and Frank jumped inside, Frank behind the steering wheel. The hatchback peeled rubber as it raced after the motorbike.

"Don't lose him!" Gina screeched as the cyclist, glancing at them over his shoulder, made a sudden left turn into a rain-drenched side street.

Slamming on the brakes, Frank swerved after him, churning up a spray of water as he sped through a complex maze of tiny streets.

"Can you make out who it is?" he called over his shoulder to Gina.

"No," she called back. "I don't think so."

"Faster!" Joe leaned forward, pointing to the left as the motorbike disappeared around another corner, sending a sheet of water into the intersection.

Veering left after the bike, Frank found that they were on a wide, straight highway. He was relieved because now the hatchback had the advantage. He stepped on the gas, easily gaining on the bike.

"Speed it up!" Joe urged, peering out the windshield and trying to identify the driver.

Clutching the steering wheel, Frank pressed harder on the accelerator. As he gained on the whining bike, he saw the cyclist glance quickly over his shoulder. For an instant his face behind the helmet was illuminated in the glare from the headlights.

"I knew it!" Joe fell back against his seat. "It's Poison! I'm sure of it!"

By now the car was so close to the bike that the spray from the bike splattered across their windshield. Alastair revved his engine and the motorbike pulled ahead slightly.

Determined, Frank gunned his engine as well. Soon the car's fender was almost touching the bike's rear wheel. A beat-up station wagon roared past from the opposite direction, blaring its horn.

"What now?" Gina squinted at the wet windshield as though it were a TV with bad reception. "How do we make him stop?"

"I think he's going to turn." Frank had seen Alastair turn his head toward a narrow road leading to the right in the distance, then aim straight ahead again. "I'll back off a little and let him do it. Then I'll corner him at the next intersection."

But as Frank eased off the accelerator, disaster struck. Alastair faked to the left as he approached the side road, then cut his wheel sharply to the right to execute the turn. But the glossy surface hid a pothole beneath the water!

Frank watched, horrified, as Alastair's front wheel hit the hole, causing the back wheel to spin out and sending a cascade of water and mud onto the hatchback's windshield.

"Wait!" Frank snapped on the windshield wipers as he went into the right turn, but the wiper only smeared mud across the glass. He hit the brakes and quickly lowered his window to try to see what was in front of the car.

It was too late. Frank felt a bump and heard the crash of metal against metal. The car went into a skid. The split second in which it spun out of control seemed like minutes to the screaming occupants of the car.

At last the car came to a stop in the center of the narrow street. Frank checked his brother and Gina. "Everyone okay?"

Miraculously, both Joe and Gina responded. In fact, Joe was out of the car before Frank could stop him. Then Frank leapt out, too. "Stay in the car!" he yelled to Gina.

Joining his brother at the scene of the accident, Frank stared at the horrible sight before them. The mangled motorbike lay upside down on the pavement, its back wheel still spinning. Frank turned to see Alastair lying ten feet away, facedown in the mud.

"There he is!" Frank yelled, running over to the prone figure.

"What is it?" Gina cried from the car. "Is he all right?"

"Stay there!" Joe shouted back. He knelt down and placed a hand on Alastair's neck.

Then his eyes met Frank's. Frank didn't like what he saw there.

"Frank."

Frank heard Joe's voice as though through a mist.

"I think we might have killed him!"

Chapter

11

"NO!" Frank bent over the figure sprawled face-down on the side of the road. Joe saw Frank's hand tremble as he reached down to feel for Alastair's pulse.

To Joe's immense relief, Alastair moaned just as Frank touched him. The biker pushed down on the muddy grass where he had landed and turned himself over.

Joe watched as Alastair's eyes focused on his brother. When he recognized Frank he jerked back, fear on his face.

"Please don't kill me!" he cried out. "I don't know nothing about the *Valiant!*"

"Nobody's out to kill you," Joe reassured him. "Just tell us why you were running from Gina's apartment."

"Later for that," Frank cautioned his brother. "We need to get him to a doctor."

"No," Alastair protested. "I—I think I'm all right." He rose to a sitting position and rubbed his head. "Just let me sit here for a moment."

Joe started to protest, but when he saw Alastair's gaze move to and rest on the mangled wreckage of his motorbike in the road, he kept his mouth shut. Instead, he stood and crossed to the totaled vehicle, righted it, and wheeled it to the side of the road. It wobbled pitifully until Joe set it down near its injured owner.

"We'll haul it back in the hatchback," he told Alastair. "Maybe you can get it fixed."

Joe heard the car door open. Gina got out and ran to the group.

"There's a hospital in Freeport," she said breathlessly. "Can he walk?"

"Yes, yes, I'm all right," Alastair protested weakly. He stood up with some assistance from Frank. Joe supported his other side, and Gina wheeled the motorbike to the car.

"We'll get you checked out at the hospital, and then we want some answers to a few questions," Joe said firmly as they limped after her.

Once Frank had managed to get Alastair into the front seat and Gina and Joe had lashed the motorbike to the car's roof rack, Gina said she'd drive and switched on the ignition. "I know the way," she insisted as she washed the mud off the windshield. "Besides, you guys have done enough tonight."

They drove for a short time along the wet streets until Joe finally spotted a ramp leading to the hospital's emergency entrance. The place looked more like a resort hotel than a hospital, Joe thought. Palm trees lined the front of the building. If it weren't for the emergency sign, he would never have noticed it.

"You get on the other side," Frank said to Joe as he helped Alastair out of the car.

"I'll park and meet you inside," Gina called, and drove off toward the lot.

The two brothers helped Alastair into the reception area. Once inside, Joe approached the gray-haired receptionist as an orderly hurried to help Alastair onto a gurney.

"Our friend has had an accident," Joe told the gray-haired receptionist. "His motorbike was totaled on a side street."

The receptionist reached for a pad. "Wheel him over here," she ordered. "I need to ask you a few questions," she said directly to Alastair.

Joe nervously watched Alastair's expression as he was wheeled up to speak to the woman. The Bahamian's face was impassive. Joe couldn't tell what he might say.

"Yes, I have insurance," Alastair calmly told the woman, and provided the necessary information. But when she asked for details of the accident, Alastair shot a sharp look at Joe.

"I hit a rut while riding my motorbike," Alastair answered. "My friends were behind me in their car. They saw the accident and helped me here."

"Good thing you were wearing that." She pointed to the black helmet Alastair still had on. "The doctor will examine you in a moment," she continued. "We'll go ahead and wheel you in."

Joe stood back as the orderly wheeled Alastair's gurney down the hall and out of view.

"Well, that was easy," Frank murmured as the two of them sat down to wait.

Joe turned as Gina entered, and he motioned to her to join them. "Yeah. But what *was* he doing at Gina's place?" he wondered.

"And why did he take off when he saw you guys coming?" Gina added.

Frank frowned. "Remember what he said to me on the road?" He looked at Joe.

"Yeah. Something about us killing him." Joe recalled the look of terror on Alastair's face.

"Why would he think that?" Gina asked.

"We were chasing him pretty hard," Frank admitted. "He might have thought he was running for his life."

"And he might have been," Joe said. "It depends on what his explanation would have been for spying on Gina!"

Joe heard footsteps coming down the hall, and he raised his eyes to see Sergeant Mylan turn the corner. The sergeant stopped as he recognized Frank and Joe, then walked slowly toward them.

"What brings you here?" he asked. "And who is your friend?"

"I'm Gina Daniels." She held out her hand.

"She works aboard the *Valiant*," Joe explained as the sergeant shook her hand. "One of the other crew members took a bad spill on his motorbike a little while ago. We're waiting for the doctor to finish his examination."

"Ah, an accident," the sergeant said almost sarcastically. "It appears crewing aboard the *Valiant* is a very unlucky occupation. And you two seem always to be around during an emergency."

"What brings *you* here, Sergeant?" Frank asked.

"I'm here tonight because of the Harry Lyman incident. His family has requested that the body be sent back to Brooklyn. I wanted to be sure forensics had all the tests it needed before I gave the okay."

"Is the verdict still the same?" Frank asked.

The sergeant hesitated. "We've decided on one more analysis before I release the body on Monday," he said. "Just a formality really, but better to do it now while we still can."

Quickly he changed the subject. "How are things on board? Any signs of treasure yet?"

"We found something interesting on Wednesday's dive," Frank told him. "The lab report should be finished by the time we start work on Monday."

"So, you have tonight and tomorrow off," Mylan observed, frowning. "Just see that you stay out of trouble."

"Yes, sir," Joe said, curbing his temper.

The little sergeant nodded and started off, his heels echoing sharply across the floor.

"I don't like the way he talked down to us," Gina remarked as the doors shut behind him.

"Look at it from his perspective," Frank pointed out. "He's had a hard day. It's after midnight, and he's probably been sweeping up after the *Valiant*'s disasters since dawn."

Joe glanced at Frank appreciatively. He, too, remembered the nights when their father, Fenton, had come home exhausted, hardly able to do more than have a bite to eat and fall into bed.

A short time later Joe spotted Alastair being pushed down the hall in a wheelchair. He was almost the old Poison again, grinning at the little group waiting for him.

"I'm not supposed to drive tonight," he announced as he joined them. "Otherwise, I'm okay."

"What a relief." Gina started for the door. "I'll bring the car around front."

"How'd you manage to avoid any broken bones?" Joe asked.

Alastair shook his head. "The doc said it must have been the soft earth I landed on. He said

I was lucky to have been thrown free of the bike.''

"Well, don't fall now," Joe said as the car arrived and he opened the door for Alastair. As the others watched, he stood unassisted, walked to the car, and eased himself into the front seat.

"Well done," Joe congratulated him as he and Frank climbed into the back. "And now that we know you're okay, we'd like to ask you a few questions."

"Yeah. Like what were you doing sneaking around my apartment?" Gina turned to glare at him for an instant.

"I wasn't sneaking around," Alastair protested. "I'd come to tell you the news. Dr. Wills showed up with the lab report on that artifact Frank found. It turned out to be some kind of tacky souvenir, probably dropped by a tourist, and Captain Delaney is in a state."

"But there were two of them, exactly alike," Frank protested. "One got knocked out of my hands and slid out of reach. What are the chances that two 'souvenirs' would have fallen into the ocean together?"

Alastair shrugged. "Dr. Wills said the carbon date tests proved it was twentieth century for sure."

"Okay, but why did you want to tell me tonight?" Gina persisted. "You could've told me on Monday, when I showed up for work."

"I overheard the captain say we'd be pulling

double shifts from now on," Alastair said mildly. "I thought you'd want to know that before you arrived on board. The rest of us would have been told tonight on ship, I'm sure."

"I can't believe it!" Gina exploded. "The crew's doing all it can now!"

"I knew you'd feel that way." Alastair's reaction was smug. "That's why I decided to let you know."

"Wait a minute," Joe interrupted. "We didn't hear you ring the doorbell. You were skulking around behind the hedges."

"I started to ring the bell," Alastair explained, "but then I saw you two coming down the stairs with Gina, and I backed away. I didn't know what to think—after all that's happened aboard ship. For all I knew, you were about to do Gina harm. So I hung around, ready to run for help if necessary."

"That was when Gina spotted me."

"Why did you run?" Joe demanded.

Alastair laughed incredulously. "How did I know you didn't mean to hurt me? My plan was to try to get someplace safe and call the ship for help."

"Why all of this sudden concern for me?" Gina asked, keeping her eyes on the road.

Alastair frowned. "I have my reasons," he said. "In fact, I have one particular reason." He reached into his front pocket. "I really think you should have this."

Joe peered through the darkness at the object in Alastair's hand. For an instant, it was illuminated by a passing street lamp. Joe heard Gina gasp. Alastair was giving her Peter's ring!

"Peter showed me many pictures of the sister he loved," Alastair said gently as Gina took the ring. "I recognized you from the start. I've done my best to look after you ever since. He gave me his ring to give to you, 'in case' was all he said."

Joe watched from the backseat, reluctant to abandon his suspicions.

"What about the Easy Life Hotel?" Joe insisted one more time. "Gina heard you mention it to Vic."

"I found a card with that name imprinted on it, and asked Vic if he knew anything about the place," Alastair explained wearily. "When you asked me about it, I didn't trust you enough to tell you anything."

"But now you trust us?" Frank asked.

Alastair smiled wryly. "Who knows? Should I?" he said. "For tonight at least, I have decided to trust you."

Gina had stopped the car in front of the dock where the *Valiant* lay at anchor, and her three companions climbed out.

"Drive home carefully," Joe cautioned her as he and Frank unloaded the motorbike onto the dock.

"I'll see you tomorrow after I've arranged for the boat," she said.

As she drove away, Joe helped Alastair up the gangplank while Frank waited with the motorbike for them to make it to the top. Frank was startled just then by a voice booming down at him from above.

"There he is!" the voice roared. "The sneak thief, trying to pull another fast one!"

On deck Joe stumbled, caught himself, and peered out into the darkness. Captain Delaney was standing at the top of the gangplank, glaring down at Frank. There was a wild expression in his eyes.

Captain Delaney must have found out that Frank had taken the marker!

"Where do you have it stashed?" the captain shouted at Frank.

"Answer me!" he roared. "I mean you, Frank Hardy!"

Chapter

12

"WHAT ARE YOU talking about?" Frank gripped the handlebars of the ruined bike.

He stared up at the enraged captain, but his mind was racing. How had Delaney discovered the missing marker? How could he explain it? For some reason Sergeant Mylan's advice came back to him: "See that you stay out of trouble."

The captain seemed to swell in size. "You made a switch, didn't you?"

Frank steeled himself. "I don't know what you mean."

"I have Dr. Wills's report on that worthless piece of junk you handed over," Captain Delaney growled threateningly.

Piece of junk? Now Frank was really confused. He raised his head to Joe to see if his brother had figured things out.

"You don't mean the—" Joe stopped just before he said the word *marker*.

"I mean the artifact you brought up this week, Frank!" the captain roared. "I saw it with my own eyes and I tell you it wasn't from the twentieth century."

Frank sagged against the motorbike, weak with relief. The captain hadn't discovered the marker after all! Next to that, his misunderstanding over the artifact seemed trivial.

But it wasn't trivial to Captain Delaney.

"Sir, you saw me turn over exactly what I found, believe me," Frank said, trying to make him see reason. "Also, I never touched the artifact after I brought it up. Poison put it in a bag, and Dr. Wills took it to the lab."

"From now on, nobody touches the net sacks once they come to the surface but Dr. Wills and myself," Delaney ordered, still blustering but with little conviction and no rage. Frank had obviously jogged his memory about the incident.

"Yes, sir." Frank let out a sigh.

"Wet suits will be taken off on deck and searched," Delaney went on. "No one aboard is going to put the integrity of this expedition in jeopardy."

"We understand, sir," Joe said, relieved as Frank made his way up the gangplank with the bike. "Whatever you say."

"I'm sure you're frustrated by the report, Captain," Frank added, leaning Poison's bike against the rail. "But I didn't have any opportunity to switch artifacts on deck. I want you to find that treasure almost as much as you do yourself."

"Well, someone switched it," the captain growled gracelessly. "For now, you can go get some sleep. But I'm keeping an eye on you." He turned to the others. "All three of you."

"Wow." Joe led Frank and Alastair to the cabins below. "I'd never seen him that mad before."

"He never felt like he lost an entire fortune before, I guess," Alastair remarked. "I don't know about you guys, but I'm glad today is over." He paused in front of his cabin door. "No hard feelings about tonight on my side."

"Not on ours, either," Joe said uncertainly. He shook Alastair's hand.

The trouble with giving up Alastair as a prime suspect, Frank realized, was that they didn't know who would replace him.

"No cracks about the breakfast, okay?" Gina said as Frank and Joe, freshly showered and refreshed, climbed into her car the next morning.

Frank examined the box of doughnuts and bottle of orange juice on the floor of the passenger seat. "Breakfast of champions," he remarked.

"Cut it out!" Gina laughed. "I've been up

since seven, arranging stuff for today. And what have you guys been doing? Sleeping. This is to eat on the way to pick up the boat.''

"What kind of boat did you rent?" Joe took the glazed doughnut Frank offered him.

"All I could get was a twelve-foot motorboat. Not much, but I figured it would do for our purposes." She accepted a doughnut from Frank, too. "I got the best wet suits and air tanks they had, but that's not saying much."

"Well, I'm up for it." Frank felt the marker and the sonar detector inside the nylon bag on his seat. "I just hope nobody sees us."

"That reminds me," Gina said. "I ran into Jason in town. He was picking up tickets for the boat races this afternoon. He said he was going to get there early for good seats."

"He must be going with Vic and Bob," Joe said. "Not a bad way to spend the day, if you don't have to cover up your brother's petty thefts."

"All right." Frank tossed a wadded-up napkin at his brother in the back seat. "I've been through enough over this so-called petty theft."

It was nine-thirty when Frank spotted the boat rental dock in Lucaya. "That's ours." Gina pointed to a four-seater that was all set to go with the gear laid out on the rear seat.

Frank nodded. Two suits, two tanks, fins, masks. "Everything seems to be in order," he said with satisfaction as Gina parked the car.

"This time, I'm driving," Joe announced as the trio walked along the pier toward the inboard. Gina sat next to him as Frank checked out the equipment in the rear. He planned to enjoy just riding for a change. The weather was spectacular—except for a few choppy waves, the storm of the night before might never have happened. It was the kind of morning he'd been looking forward to.

"Do you know how to find the spot?" Frank heard Gina ask Joe as the boat bounced over the waves.

"I can locate it by sight," Joe shouted over the engine. "I memorized some landmarks last time we were there."

Frank gazed out at the area where he'd found the marker. Several boats dotted the water, and one in particular seemed anchored right about where they were going. Frank watched it idly for a moment, then sat up straight.

"That's funny," he shouted.

Gina turned to look at him.

"As soon as we started heading toward that boat, it pulled anchor and moved off."

"Maybe they thought we were crowding them," Gina suggested.

Frank didn't see how. There was more than enough room for everyone, but he said nothing. By the time Joe cut the ignition, Frank was already climbing into his wet suit.

Joe began getting into his suit while Gina took his place at the wheel.

"Remember, keep your eye on the shoreline," he instructed as he suited up. "Pick out a landmark—"

"Joe, you're talking to a marine archaeologist," she reminded him. "I think I can handle a boat alone."

"Just checking." Joe grinned, embarrassed.

Meanwhile, Frank dug out a rope from under the backseat and tied one end to a metal hook on the port side. He got out a lead weight and tied it to the other end so the line would sink to the bottom.

"We can use this as a signaling device," he explained. "We'll give it a tug if anything goes wrong below. Gina can do the same topside."

Gina nodded.

"We each have an hour's worth of air," Frank continued, taking the marker and the sonar detector box out of his nylon duffel. "I think two twenty-minute dives should do it, but we'll have extra air if we have to go down again."

Gina seemed to be a little concerned. "Be careful down there, both of you," she said.

"We will." Joe saluted her. Then he and his brother went over the side.

As always, Frank was amazed by the beauty of the underwater world as he slipped beneath the surface. Breathing slowly, he gazed through his mask at the dark blue water and exotic fish.

He checked out Joe, who also seemed enchanted by the view.

As they sank slowly down to the ocean floor, Frank grabbed the line that dangled from their boat and handed it to Joe. Joe gave it an experimental tug, got one back, and signaled thumbs-up to his brother.

About twenty yards to the left of their landing site Frank recognized the area he'd explored before. In the past few days the shifting sands had begun to disguise the ocean floor, but the deep chasm was unmistakable. Frank swam slowly along one edge, trying to get his bearings.

Ten minutes later Frank came upon the marker he'd left where he had found the pair of identical objects. Following his trail backward, he swam along the edge of the chasm to the place where he'd found the white, sonar-equipped cube.

This is easier than I'd expected, Frank thought as he replaced the sonarless marker with the original one. Joe hovered to one side, keeping one hand on the signal line.

Once the marker was in place Frank felt a huge surge of relief. He hadn't realized how uncomfortable he'd been knowing that at any moment the person who planted the sonars might discover one was missing.

Frank decided to see what lay in the opposite direction. He tapped Joe's shoulder and indicated that he should follow.

At first it seemed a waste of time. None of

the outcroppings appeared to be remarkable, and without the Air Lift it was difficult to sort out the different barnacle-covered shapes.

Frank was about to return to his original course when Joe signaled him.

Frank swam after his brother and peered down at the place Joe indicated. Excited, he turned and gave the thumbs-up sign to Joe.

Jutting up from the sand was another one of the white markers. Frank lifted it up in the water. He nodded exaggeratedly. It seemed heavy. He'd bet anything it concealed a sonar.

They swam on, faster now, heading in the same direction. Soon Joe spotted another white marker lying in the sand. He showed it to Frank, who inspected it and nodded again.

These led in the opposite direction from the trail the *Valiant* has been following, Frank observed. Apparently, someone knows—or thinks he knows—where the sunken treasure really is. And that someone is keeping it a secret.

Frank pondered this as he and Joe continued following the markers. He knew that in one more week Captain Delaney would be out of funds. Could it be that the captain was deliberately misleading the crew so he wouldn't have to share the profits with them after the week was over? If so, did he dive alone to set up the markers? Or was he working with someone? One of the crew members? Or was there another explanation? Frank's mind reeled with possibilities.

Joe caught Frank's eye and pointed to his watch. They'd told Gina they'd be down only twenty minutes on the first dive. Frank realized they'd been down twenty-five already.

Though he hated to tear himself away from the trail of sonar, Frank gave Joe the okay sign and started to adjust the valve in his BC jacket. He raised his eyes to the tether Joe held in his hand—and felt as though his heart had stopped beating!

Frank reached out slowly, grabbing Joe's shoulder, and began shaking it.

Puzzled, Joe followed Frank's finger pointing up.

A black shape hovered high above their heads, then all at once began spiraling down toward them.

Frank shook Joe's shoulder harder. Joe squinted against the sunlight that pierced the water's surface.

The shape was vaguely familiar.

Then all too soon it became extremely familiar.

Circling down upon them, with its jaws agape, was an enormous shark!

Chapter

13

NOOOO! The silent scream echoed in Joe's head. He stared up at the shark, willing himself not to panic. He yanked on the rope, signaling Gina that something was wrong. Beyond that, he could do nothing, yet. Unarmed, Joe knew they were no match for the beast.

In the instant before the shark arrived, everything Joe had ever read about them passed through his mind in a blur. If only we'd brought spear guns, he thought desperately. At least an electric prod! Sharks hadn't been a problem in the dives off the *Valiant* because they usually didn't swim so close to shore—at least that was what he'd thought.

The shark was no more than fifteen yards away. Come up with something—fast! Joe told himself. He looked over at Frank, who was treading water, moving slowly one way, then the other.

Suddenly Joe's head cleared and logic took over. The sonar detector!

Joe spotted it hanging from Frank's belt. He signaled his brother to use it. At first, Frank didn't seem to understand. Then, just as the shark swam closer to Joe than Frank was himself, he understood.

Just count to ten, Joe said to himself, bracing himself against a mound of rock as he waited for the shark's first attack. He watched intently as Frank fumbled with his equipment belt, managed to unclip the sonar, and held it tightly in his hand.

Eight, seven, six . . .

Frank pushed the sonar detector's red button, but to Joe's horror, nothing happened. Then Frank realized his mistake. He swam closer to one of the markers and prepared to try again.

Five, four . . . By now the shark was close enough for Joe to see the rows of teeth inside its gaping jaw. Why me? Joe wondered briefly as he gripped the communications rope and got ready to fight for his life.

Once again Frank pressed the sonar button.

At first the ploy had no effect.

But then suddenly the attacking giant faltered, confused. Inches from Joe's torso, it veered away and drifted several yards to the left.

Joe had just started to relax when the shark rallied and circled for another attack.

Ten. Joe stood motionless as the beast charged him for the second time. But again it veered at the last instant and swam past him.

Joe watched it go. It headed for the marker, churning the waters of the ocean's sandy bottom in a wild attempt to get to the device.

Frank backed off quickly, signaling Joe to break for the surface. Joe held on to the rope as they made their ascent, hoping the shark's attraction to the marker would last long enough for them to make it to the boat safely.

Never thought I'd see that again, he admitted to himself as the boat's outline became visible on the surface. He swam steadily right behind Frank, not daring to look back as he raced to safety.

Alerted by Joe's frantic pulls on the rope, Gina waited with the rope ladder at the side of the boat. "What happened?" she cried as Frank and Joe broke the surface of the water. She reached out to Joe and helped pull him onto the boat.

"Shark!" was all Joe could say.

Gina gasped. She helped pull Frank out of the water, just as the shark's fin broke the surface a short distance away.

"Wow." Gina stared at the enormous fin as the brothers pulled off their equipment, gasping for breath. They watched it cut through a wave not ten yards from the boat. Joe sat, awestruck at how close disaster had been.

"We'll have to remember to tell Dan Fields about that one," Joe finally said as the shark swam away.

Gina still looked shaken. "Are you both all right?"

"Sure." Frank appeared as calm as ever. He held the black sonar detector up for Joe to see. "That makes the second time this little device you wanted to leave at the airport has come in handy," he pointed out smugly.

"Hey, let's not forget I was the one who remembered that article about the World War Two navy experiments."

"What experiments?" Gina asked.

"The navy was testing sonar as a possible shark repellent," Joe explained. "But it turned out that, instead of being repelled by it, the sharks were attracted to the sound. They can't get enough of it, in fact."

"You mean that monster passed up your tasty limbs for some boring electrical impulses?" Gina teased.

"You could put it that way," Joe said.

"We haven't told you the good news yet," Frank added. "We found a trail of sonars down there. I'll bet they lead straight to the *Doña Bonita!*"

"So someone really has secretly marked out a path." Gina frowned. "But who?"

"Someone who wants it all for himself." Joe unzipped the jacket of his wet suit and gazed out over the water.

The shark, still in the area, was lunging through the water, its huge jaws still open. Joe frowned, watching more closely. The beast seemed to be in a feeding frenzy.

"What's going on?" he asked nobody in particular.

Frank was also watching the shark's movements, but his gaze shifted slightly and he peered at the water a short distance from the boat.

"Why didn't I notice that before?" he said. He pointed to a number of dark shapes floating just beneath the waves. As one surfaced, Joe saw that it was a hunk of meat drifting in the current.

"Whoever left that trail down below really wants to discourage visitors," Frank said grimly. "He's baited the water to attract sharks. It's amazing there aren't more around."

"Remember the boat that pulled away as we approached the site?" Joe asked.

Frank nodded. "I guess whoever it was didn't want us to get close enough to recognize him."

"Shouldn't we head back in?" Gina asked. "With that shark circling, there's no way we can do any more diving today."

The brothers agreed, and Joe began hauling in the rope they had used as a tether. He had pulled in only about three yards when he held the end up in the air. "Look at this," he said. The shark had neatly severed the rope at that point!

"That could have been one of our legs," Joe said, staring at the ragged end of rope.

"As it is, there goes part of our deposit," Frank joked weakly. Joe grinned, but he noticed that Gina didn't crack a smile.

"Thirty dollars!" Joe complained when the rental clerk subtracted the cost of the rope from their deposit. "That's highway robbery!"

"Piracy's more like it," Gina commented dryly, leading them to her car. "But a small price to pay, considering it might have saved your lives."

She checked Frank for a reaction, but the older Hardy appeared to be lost in thought. "I know," she said. "One more favor, right?"

Frank looked surprised as they climbed into the hatchback. "I was just wondering whether I could borrow one of your newspaper clippings about the *Valiant*. The one with the picture of the crew."

"Sure, but why?" Gina turned the key in the ignition.

"Just a hunch," Frank told her. "Also, I was hoping Joe and I could borrow your car for a few hours."

"You want to go somewhere without me?"

"Where to?" Joe asked from the back seat.

"I want to pay another visit to Waves. I just hope Max Trepo hangs out there as much as I think he does."

As they waited in the car for Gina to return with the newspaper clipping, Joe wondered what his brother was up to. Frank was in one of those moods, Joe observed, in which he refused to share his suspicions with anyone.

I hate it when he's like this, Joe thought gloomily. After that encounter with the shark, all his own theories about disappearances and thefts seemed to have flown out the window. All he wanted now was to eat lunch and sleep.

"Here you go." Gina handed Frank the clipping through the open window. "Sure I can't come with you?"

"Thanks." Frank avoided her question. Joe knew his brother thought Waves was too dangerous for them to bring Gina along, but he didn't want to tell her so. "We'll be back soon," he added, putting the car into gear.

Joe waved as Gina stepped back onto the sidewalk.

When the green hatchback pulled into the parking lot at Waves, Joe counted only eight or ten cars parked there. "Look." He pointed at Max's black car with the tinted windows. "Our hero's arrived before us."

"I figured," Frank said with obvious satisfaction. "Guys like Max have to hang around places like this all day. It's the only way they can feel in charge."

Joe was disappointed at how run-down the club really was. In the daylight it resembled a truck stop, Joe decided, and a shabby one at that.

Once inside, Joe immediately spotted Max sitting in a booth, reading the paper.

"Hey, Max," Frank said, sitting down across the table from the skinny man. "Any luck setting up that meeting with Pete Duvall?"

Max turned his head to stare at him through half-closed lids. He didn't seem a bit surprised to see them there, Joe noted. "I'm waiting for his call now," Max told them. "That's why I'm hanging out."

"You sure he'll call?" Joe mumbled.

"Would I be here if I wasn't?" Max snarled. "I'm busy. You boys come back tonight like we planned."

Joe watched Max go back to reading the paper. He could sense that Frank was about to put his plan into action—whatever his plan might be.

"Yeah, Duvall has some nerve, keeping a guy like you hanging," Frank said smoothly, shooting a look to Joe.

"He sure does," Joe drawled, picking up the salt shaker and playing with it. "He's going to be on easy street, raking in all the big bucks, while we're out a grand and you're out on bail, waiting to be sentenced.''

Joe hid his amusement as he saw Max's face redden at the thought.

"It makes me sore the way some guys think they can use other people," Joe heard Frank observe beside him.

"Yeah." Joe set the salt shaker down. "Like some people get off scot-free, loaded with dough. While other guys spend some of their best years locked up in jail."

"We'll take care of him tonight." Max slapped the paper with the palm of his hand.

"Good. Because guys like that need to be taught a lesson," Joe went on. He hoped he wasn't hamming it up too much. "Otherwise they think they can spend their lives hanging out with the society crowd, throwing their money around while the rest of us rot out here in the boonies."

Joe flashed a quick look at Max. The crook was squirming uncomfortably in the booth. Joe figured his blood pressure must be rising.

"You're right," Frank said, pressing harder now. "Look, our guy even gets his picture in the paper like he's some kind of hero, just because he's diving for some sunken wreck." He laid the newspaper article on the table in front of Max. "And what did he do when he found the treasure? He sold it to you and sent you to the clink!"

119

Joe was sure the tactic had worked. Max was in a rage now. "He doesn't know who he's fooling with," the crook grumbled. He turned his attention to the photo, speaking directly to it. "I'll see you get what's coming to you, buddy. First thing tonight!" Max jabbed his finger at Peter's image.

There was only one thing wrong.

Joe glanced at his brother, then back at the paper. There was no mistake. Max Trepo was pointing to Jason Matthews!

Chapter

14

"THAT'S PETER DUVALL?" Frank asked, pointing to Jason's image in the photo.

"Sure!" Max exclaimed. "Hey, hold on a minute. I thought you said you knew him."

Frank looked at his brother. He couldn't believe his ears. So it was Jason who'd been behind it all along! He stood up abruptly.

"Thanks, pal. You've been a great help," he said, pumping Max's hand. The small-time hood stared blankly after him as he and Joe left the club.

On the way to Gina's, Frank silently celebrated while Joe tried to put it all together. "It must have been Jason who phoned Max at Waves, telling him we were on our way there to give him trouble."

"And he baited the water out by our diving

121

site. That's what he was up to in Lucaya when Gina ran into him this morning," Frank added. "He must have guessed we'd go to the site and waited there until he saw us."

"Now all we have to do is find him," Joe said grimly.

"Wait a minute, Joe. He couldn't have done everything on his own. One of the other crew members has to be in on it with him."

"And there's still the question of what happened to Peter Duvall," Joe said.

Frank didn't like the answer that came immediately to mind. So he changed the subject. "Unless I miss my guess, Jason is probably about to clear out. He knows we're onto him. There's no way he's going to stick around." Frank rounded the corner onto Gina's street.

They parked out front and rang Gina's bell. As she opened the door, Frank saw that she'd changed clothes and was brushing her hair, which was damp.

"Good thing you got back early," she said. "I need the car to run some errands."

"Can you drop us off at the *Valiant* first?" Frank asked. "We just received some information that we need to look into."

"Let me get my wallet." A moment later she had joined the boys and was following them back to the car.

"Is this all top secret or are you going to let me in on it?" Gina asked as the car flew down the road toward the docks. "Have you found out something more about Peter?"

"As soon as we're sure, we'll tell you all about it," Frank promised.

Gina was disappointed, he noted, but he was relieved that she didn't question him further.

Ten minutes later Frank and Joe got out of the car at the dock. "My errands shouldn't take long," Gina called as they headed for the ship. "I'll be back in half an hour."

"She's determined to find out what we know," Joe warned his brother.

"I know," said Frank. "And I wish I didn't have to tell her."

He raised his eyes to the *Valiant*. It appeared to be deserted. Frank led the way to the cabins.

"Time for a major confrontation," he told Joe as they neared Jason's cabin. Frank heard noises coming from behind the open door.

Frank peered inside. Jason was hurriedly stuffing his things into a bag. His room was a mess. Drawers hung open, and clothes were scattered about. A torn and crumpled letter lay on the bed beside the suitcase.

"Going somewhere?" Frank's voice startled Jason. He turned, and a look of desperation crossed his face.

"We had a little chat with Max Trepo a while ago," Frank said calmly. "He identified a photo of you as being Peter Duvall."

"We also want to thank you for introducing

us to some of the larger forms of sea life in the Bahamas,'' Joe added sarcastically.

"I don't know what you're talking about." Jason continued cramming things into his bag. "Anyway, I'm leaving. The captain says the lab report on the artifact y'all found came back negative. This little expedition is headed nowhere."

"But the captain has only Dr. Wills's word on the lab report, doesn't he?" Frank tried to make the dark-haired boy meet his gaze.

Jason refused. His eyes flickered about the room, searching for a way out.

Keeping his eye on Jason, Frank picked the crumpled piece of paper up off the bed. It seemed to have been torn in half. Frank separated the two halves and inspected them.

"Leave that alone!" Jason lunged for the paper. "That's none of your business!"

Joe held Jason back as Frank read the note aloud. " 'Dear Gina, Just a note to tell you I think I'm really onto something aboard the *Valiant*. I'm convinced that a couple of the crew are trying to sabotage Captain Delaney's mission and wind up with everything for themselves. I think I have the proof, too! I can't tell you any more, because if anything happens to me I want you to . . .' "

The note was torn at that point. It appeared to Frank that a sentence or two had been removed.

But Joe remembered the day at the Easy Life Hotel and the note they'd found on the windshield. Speaking in a monotone, he filled in the missing line. " 'Keep out of this. Believe me you won't be able to handle it.' "

Frank stared at him. Then he finished reading the rest of Peter's letter. " 'Remember, I love you and can't wait to see you and the folks soon. Peter.' "

Frank saw that Joe was boiling mad. He grabbed the southerner by the shirt. "All right, you slime," he growled, "what happened to Gina's brother?"

Frantic, Jason reached out for the suitcase to swing up toward Joe's chin. Joe avoided the blow but did let go of Jason in the process. "Get him!" he yelled to his brother as Jason rushed out the door.

Frank charged after the lanky young man, but Jason turned and flung the bag in Frank's direction.

Frank ducked as the bag hit the wall behind him. He made a flying leap for Jason, knocking him to the floor in the passageway.

"All right!" Joe rushed over and yanked Jason to his feet, slipping his arms under the Southerner's shoulders in a viselike grip.

"I asked you a question." Joe's face was red with anger. "What happened to Peter Duvall?"

The pain made it hard for Jason to answer. He struggled, trying to free himself from Joe's grasp. Joe pulled him back into his cabin.

Once inside Frank walked around to address

the guy face-to-face. "We know you had to be working with someone else," he said, making Jason look him in the eye. "I've got a pretty good idea who it is. But if you want, we can let the police straighten this out."

"I don't think either of you boys is going to do much talking to the police after we get through with you."

Frank tensed. He knew without turning around that the voice belonged to Dr. Benjamin Wills.

"I wondered whether you were still around," Frank said, keeping all traces of emotion out of his voice.

"Yes, I'm still here. But I'm afraid we won't be able to say the same for you two in a little while."

Although Frank's back was to the doctor, he could see his reflection in the mirror on the door of the shower. Dr. Wills held a medical bag in his left hand, and in his right was a .38 revolver aimed straight at Frank's head.

"Now, Joe, why don't you let go of my friend and sit over there on the bed?" Wills said softly. "Go on, both of you!" He gestured to the bed with the weapon.

Joe released his grip on Jason. He and Frank moved over to the bed. Jason stood next to the doctor, rubbing his neck and shoulders.

"The police know all about this, you know," Frank said loudly. "We talked with Sergeant Mylan after our meeting with the shark this morning. He's probably on his way here right now."

"All the more reason to take care of you quickly and clear out for good," Dr. Wills responded with a sinister smile.

Frank knew the doctor's tone was infuriating Joe. "You'll never get off the island," Joe said to them. "The police will check the docks and the airport."

"Perhaps you've forgotten about my private plane, my friend. There are private runways all over this island."

Frank let out his breath. The doctor had his escape worked out pretty well. Frank wondered whether Gina would show up soon—or a minute too late.

"I want to know what you did with Peter Duvall," Frank insisted, stalling for time. "Where is he?"

Dr. Wills only laughed. "Jason, take this." He handed the gun to him. "If they try anything, shoot to kill."

"I asked about Peter Duvall," Frank reminded the doctor as Jason proudly took over his assignment, pointing the weapon at the Hardys.

"I'm afraid Mr. Duvall got to be a major nuisance to us," Dr. Wills said. "He was snooping around, like you two, and he found out too much."

"Where is he?" Joe shouted, red-faced. Frank put a hand on his brother's arm to restrain him.

"Floating out in the channel somewhere

between here and Nassau." Jason laughed as though it were a great joke.

Frank's stomach tightened. He had feared that might be the case, but up to now he had hoped that he was wrong.

"We'll never be able to tell her." Joe could barely speak the words.

"Don't worry," Dr. Wills said, setting his medical bag on the bed and sitting next to it. "Neither of you will be in any condition to do any talking about anything, to anyone, anymore."

Frank stared at the black bag. "I guess that's how you killed Harry Lyman, isn't it?" he said. "I remember when he came back from his physical, he held his hand under his arm."

"You're very observant and very clever." Dr. Wills opened the bag. "Observant enough to know he was probably given a shot under the arm, where the hair follicles help conceal any needle marks from the coroner's examination."

Frank faced the doctor. "I've also figured out that a shot of potassium chloride will produce a fatal arrhythmia, or heart attack."

"You amaze me," Dr. Wills said, studying each of them in turn. "Too bad that such vast knowledge has only landed you in this, shall we say, unfortunate situation."

Frank watched Dr. Wills open the bag and take out a syringe and two ampules. "The choice of potassium chloride was a good one." Dr. Wills looked at Frank. "Don't you think?"

"Yes," Frank said bitterly. "After a dive, the body naturally produces a greater supply of potassium in the bloodstream. During the autopsy, the coroner wouldn't find it unusual to find large amounts if the victim had dived that day."

"A-plus!" Dr. Wills broke off the seal on the syringe and inserted it into one of the small vials.

"Why can't we let them have it with this?" Jason asked, waving the gun.

"Too noisy," the doctor said. "Gunshots could attract unwanted guests who might get in the way of our escape."

"Harry found out about the sonar and the way you were leading Captain Delaney astray with the search, didn't he?" Joe asked, knowing the answer already.

"I think you boys have learned enough for one day." Wills stared at Frank, and his tone changed. "Roll up your sleeve," he ordered.

Frank glanced at Joe, whose forehead was creased. He must have been trying to think of some way to help. Then his gaze switched to Jason, who smirked as he crossed to the doorway for a better view, keeping the gun pointed at them.

Dr. Wills assumed a mock bedside manner as he poised the needle over Frank's arm.

"Just relax," he said softly, positioning his thumb on the plunger. "This won't hurt a bit."

Chapter

15

JOE WATCHED HELPLESSLY as Dr. Wills aimed the syringe filled with a lethal dose of potassium chloride at Frank's arm. What now? he asked himself. I've got to do something!

Just then the room exploded with the noise of a gun being fired. A wild bullet came from nowhere, narrowly missing Joe's head and hitting the wall behind him.

"What—" Dr. Wills looked up in time to see Jason fall to the floor, his gun skittering across it.

Joe realized that Alastair had burst into the room and had tackled Jason from behind. He must have been listening in the hallway, Joe thought excitedly as the crewman subdued the lanky Southerner.

Frank landed a single neat uppercut on Dr.

Wills's jaw, then Joe went after him and pulled him away from his brother.

"Frank!" It was Alastair. Jason was beginning to get the better of their fight.

As Joe held off the flailing doctor, Frank went over to help Alastair with Jason, who had his right leg drawn up to deliver a deadly kick to the floored Bahamian's head.

"The gun, Frank!" Joe shouted.

But the gun had slid under the edge of the bed, out of Frank's reach. Joe landed a solid right cross on Wills's chin, knocking him backward and offering Joe a quick glimpse of Frank blocking Jason's kick to Alastair. As Wills staggered to his feet again, Frank flipped Jason backward, while Alastair rolled into a ball and spun free.

Joe turned toward Alastair, and Wills took advantage of the moment to land a right hook to Joe's left temple. Joe cried out and stumbled backward, his head reeling.

As he fell, Joe became vaguely aware of Alastair making a dive for the gun.

"Wait a minute," Joe mumbled weakly, but it was too late.

Jason had thrown Frank off and was now leaping over Joe for the gun as well.

Joe fought for consciousness as Alastair and Jason both reached for the weapon at the same time. In Joe's confusion, the gun seemed to be an inch or two in front of his nose. He stood up shakily, knocking the gun across the floor with his foot, and lurched toward Dr. Wills.

"Where'd it go?" Jason staggered after the missing gun, but he failed to reach it. Joe pulled back to smash Wills's face with his fist just as Frank made a flying leap, landing on Jason with all the force of a steamroller.

The Southerner's wind was knocked out of him as Frank pulled him to his feet and delivered a final blow to his midsection.

"That way, Frank!" Joe yelled as he ducked one of Dr. Wills's killer rights, then grabbed the doctor's extended hand and, with all his remaining energy, threw him to the ground.

Wills fell to the floor like a rag doll. Joe swayed above him, while Alastair cried out, "The gun, on the floor near you!"

Joe looked down to see the gun spinning at his feet. It reminded him of a hockey puck. Dulled by the fighting, he kicked it over to Alastair.

Alastair picked up the revolver and held it on the two thieves. Frank and Joe relaxed, trying to catch their breath.

Finally Joe spoke. "I think there are a couple of cells with your names on them at the jailhouse in Freeport."

"But I'm afraid your stay will probably last longer than overnight," Frank added.

"Come on, fellas," Wills said nervously. "Let's keep this just between us. There'll be more than enough gold for everyone to share."

"Yeah, we know," Frank said. "That's why Captain Delaney agreed to share it. He wanted all the people who helped find the *Doña Bonita* to get rich."

Joe tried to control his temper. "No deals, Wills," he said. "The only deals you'll make from now on will be with a deck of cards—playing solitaire in your cell."

Jason slumped down onto the bed, his hands covering his face. "You told me it was a foolproof plan," he moaned.

"Listen to reason," Dr. Wills pleaded with Joe.

To show him they meant business Joe crossed over to where the needle and vial now lay on the floor. He brought his foot down, grinding them into the floor with his shoe.

"Poison, keep that gun aimed right where it is. We're going to pay a visit to Sergeant Mylan. I think he'll be glad to see this case wrapped up," Frank said calmly.

"All right, you two, start walking." Alastair spat out the order.

Dr. Wills glanced at the .38, then started slowly for the cabin door. Jason followed the doctor, his eyes fastened on the floor.

Alastair went out next, with Frank behind him. Joe paused just long enough to gather the shredded halves of Peter Duvall's letter. He thought of Gina and felt queasy again. He dreaded having to tell her about her brother's death.

133

"Just keep walking and go up the companion-way. Don't try anything foolish," he heard Frank say. Joe hurried to catch up with them.

The passage was too narrow to walk three abreast, so the group marched toward the stairs in single file.

As Dr. Wills reached the bottom step, Joe heard footsteps on the deck above. "Gina!" he called.

"Joe, are you down there?" Gina appeared at the top of the stairs. "Is everything all right?"

She started down the stairs when she realized that Alastair was holding a gun. "What's going on?" she said sharply.

"Get out of here!" Joe bellowed. But it was too late.

Dr. Wills lunged forward and grabbed Gina's arm, pulling her in front of him to use like a shield. Joe gasped. Wills now had Gina between him and Alastair!

"Don't shoot!" Frank yelled. He and Joe watched helplessly as Jason lunged up the steps, too, and positioned himself behind the doctor and Gina.

"Well, things seem to have taken a turn for the better. For us, anyway, wouldn't you say?" Jason said, taunting the Hardys.

Joe itched to make a move for Wills, but he was too far back in line. Frank started forward, but Wills had anticipated that.

"One more step and I'll snap her back in two like a matchstick," Wills said, his eyes ablaze.

"You hurt her and I'll—" Joe's face flushed red with anger.

"You're in no position to give warnings, my friend." Dr. Wills gave the words a cruel edge. "Poison, toss the gun down the hall to my friend Jason, or I'll show you all how easy it is to crack a spinal column in two. Believe me, I'm fully prepared to demonstrate if you choose not to cooperate," he threatened.

Dr. Wills inched down the companionway toward the trio, shoving Gina ahead of him. Alastair looked to the Hardys for help.

"I'm not joking." The doctor increased the pressure on Gina's arm, which he held twisted behind her. "Do as I say or so help me, I'll keep my promise."

"Do it!" Joe snapped at Alastair.

The Bahamian hesitated but finally bent close to the floor and slid the revolver down the passageway. It came to rest at Jason's feet.

"Now you're behaving sensibly," Wills said.

Once Jason had his hands on the .38, Dr. Wills shoved Gina down the last two steps and into the trio before him. Joe saw Frank's arms reach out to steady her.

"It's time you did some marching," the doctor said through his teeth. "Get back into Jason's cabin, all of you!"

The group turned around and walked back

toward the small room. These might be the last moments of my life, Joe couldn't help thinking. It was hard to believe. He tried to remember why he had pleaded with his father to let him take this job.

"Empty your pockets," the doctor said. "Throw everything on the bed." He seemed in a hurry now. After they complied, the doctor scanned their belongings, taking only the keys from each pile.

"This is a waste of time. Let's just let them have it with this!" Jason said, holding the revolver out in front of him.

"No need for that. I have a better idea." Dr. Wills pocketed the keys, glancing regretfully at the smashed hypo and vial on the floor. "That would have been the perfect solution," he admitted. "But no matter. Go to the lounge quickly and get all the magazines and newspapers you can find," he ordered Jason.

Jason was confused. The doctor continued, "On your way back, litter the hallway with them. It's a bit chilly in here. I think we could use a little fire to warm things up, don't you?"

Joe stared at his brother and then at Gina, who seemed to be in shock, unable to believe her ears.

But Jason seemed pleased as he ran out the door to carry out his orders.

"All right, everyone on the floor," Dr. Wills said, backing toward the doorway. "You'll only be uncomfortable for a little while, until the fire reaches the fuel tank. Then it'll all be over in a flash.''

Joe could hear Jason spreading the paper down the hallway as Dr. Wills backed out of the room. He glanced over at Gina, whose face was almost expressionless with terror.

Joe peeked back over his shoulder. At the open doorway, Dr. Wills had stopped and taken a book of matches from his pocket. He checked out the cabin one last time, making sure there was no chance of escape.

Then he handed the matches to Jason, turned, and left.

Joe could only watch helplessly as Jason gazed at the four captives and laughed. Joe shuddered. He had heard laughs that crazy before, but he had never been on the losing end of one. As he watched, Jason struck a match and held it aloft, savoring the moment.

"So long, suckers," Jason said, flicking the match onto the pile of papers. Then he slowly closed and locked the cabin door.

Instantly Joe and the other prisoners started moving around the cabin, searching for a way out.

But Joe knew it was no use. His eyes met Gina's. She, too, knew there was no escape.

Any moment the fire would reach the fuel tank, and the entire ship would explode!

Chapter

16

"THE PORTHOLE!"

Frank responded to Gina's suggestion as though it were a command. He ran to the single porthole in the room. But it was only a foot in diameter. Even Gina, Frank knew, would never be able to squeeze through.

Think, Frank told himself. He knew they were losing valuable time. While they were trapped inside this inferno, Dr. Wills and Jason were making their escape.

"This door is solid steel," Frank heard Joe yell. He looked over to see his brother pressing his weight against the door. His gaze faltered, then fell on the bookcase next to the door frame.

Something about a bookcase, he told himself vaguely. What was it? A door? Harry's room?

Startled, Frank approached his brother.

"The ice pick!" he shouted.

"What?" Joe stared at him as though he'd gone mad.

"The ice pick!" Frank yelled, pounding the door. "Harry used it when he locked himself in!"

Joe's jaw dropped open. "Brother," he said, "you've just saved all our lives. Let's hope all the cabin doors on this ship are equipped with the same safety release."

Kneeling to inspect the latch mechanism, Joe crowed in triumph. "This one does!" he shouted. "But what do we use for a pick?"

"There has to be something here," Frank said, moving toward the closet. But Gina stopped him, guessing what he was looking for.

"It's stripped bare," she informed him. "Not one hanger on the rod."

The smoke was growing dense in the room. This was insane. There had to be something they could use to set themselves free.

"Is there anything on that scrap heap?" Joe asked, gesturing toward the piles of belongings from their pockets, which had been laid out on the bed.

Frank stared at the items. His eyes widened. He picked up Alastair's ballpoint pen, which lay half hidden by the edge of the blanket.

"I already thought of that," said Alastair, coughing from the smoke that was filling the room. "It's too wide to fit into the tiny opening."

"But the ink tube isn't." Frank unscrewed the cap of the pen and was at the door by the time he finished speaking.

"I may have to force it, but I think it'll work!" he exclaimed. It was a a tight fit, but the metal tube finally penetrated the chamber. Frank kept inserting it until the tube met with some resistance. Then he gave it one more push, and heard something click inside.

The others cheered wildly as Frank wrapped the end of his shirt around the searing-hot handle and twisted it to the right. The door swung open! But the group's joy was short-lived as flames entered the cabin.

"Strip the blankets," Frank snapped. Joe quickly obeyed. The brothers gathered Alastair and Gina underneath the blankets and headed toward the door.

As they moved through the doorway, Frank said, "Make a run for it, and whatever you do, don't stop along the way!"

Crouching as low to the ground as possible, the group ran in single file. Frank guided them through the smoke from memory, feeling his way to the companionway. It was only when they reached the top that Frank threw off the smoldering blankets and tossed them out into the water.

"The fire extinguisher!" Alastair coughed as

he spoke. "There's one on this deck." He raced toward it before they could stop him.

"No, wait!" Frank called. "You can't fight that thing alone!" But Alastair was already on his way back with the red canister.

"The fire's still mainly feeding on the paper!" the Bahamian shouted. "If I can't handle it, I'll get out of there fast!" he assured Frank. "You two go on after Dr. Wills and Jason. They're getting away!"

Frank turned in time to spot the doctor and Jason leaping into a cabin cruiser halfway down the dock. He signaled Joe to follow as he ran for the gangplank. Gina started after them.

"Stay here," Joe ordered, turning to her. "Better yet, go notify the police!"

As he raced down the dock, Frank saw the cabin cruiser pull out of its berth and head out into the channel. He wondered where the doctor and Jason were going. Wills's private plane could be anywhere, but it was a short boat ride to the Freeport airport.

He saw that Jason was waving his gun and ducked down behind a boat in a nearby berth. A middle-aged couple was unloading fishing equipment from the boat onto the nearby dock. Frank eyed the couple in amazement. Didn't they see him, trying not to get shot by hiding ten feet away?

"Keep your heads down. There may be some shooting!" Frank called to the couple, but the blaring Caribbean dance music on their ship's radio drowned out his voice. Frank stepped out to warn them again.

That proved to be a major mistake. Jason saw him, aimed the .38, and fired two shots as the boat surged forward into the channel.

"Hit the ground!" Joe yelled, running up behind Frank.

Frank dropped facedown onto the wooden planks as bullets rang over his head. To his right, the screaming middle-aged couple dove into the shadow of their two-seater.

"Stay down!" Frank yelled as more bullets rang out from the motorboat. One lodged in the dock halfway between Frank's head and the woman's foot. She screamed. Then Frank had an idea.

"Untie the stern!" he yelled to his brother, checking to see that the couple's keys were in the boat's ignition.

"Great," he murmured when he saw them. He leapt into the driver's seat, relieved to note that the boat was backed into the berth so that it faced out into the channel. As Joe untied the lines, Frank turned the ignition. "Get in!" he yelled to Joe.

"What do you two think you're doing?" the boat's owner raged, grabbing Joe by the collar.

In one quick movement Joe threw up his arms, freeing himself from the man's grasp, and knocked him to the ground. The man's wife screamed at the top of her lungs.

"Sorry, no time to explain now!" Frank said, moving over as Joe took over the throttle. He pushed it all the way down and the motorboat lurched forward.

"They have a big lead," Frank shouted as Joe shifted into high gear, chasing the fleeing craft.

"Water's choppy," Joe observed.

Frank eyed the white caps atop the waves as the boat slammed down into them after each bounce. "Doesn't matter. We're gaining on them," he muttered to himself. The Hardys' boat, though not engineered for speed, had an edge over Wills's cabin cruiser. Frank held on tight as they bounded over the cruiser's wake.

"Uh-oh," Joe yelled. "They've recognized us." The Hardys ducked as Jason fired another wild shot in their direction.

"We'll never be able to get close enough to stop them while he still has that thirty-eight!" Frank yelled.

"Let's hope they don't have any more ammunition. He's already fired four shots," Joe shouted back.

Just ahead of the cabin cruiser Frank saw a number of small, sleek craft scattered along the channel. "Racing boats!" he shouted. Sprays of water dissolved in the air as the racers made hairpin turns around a line of buoys marking their route.

Joe couldn't help but grin with excitement. "The international speedboat competition! Wills is going to have to fight his way through that if he wants to get to the Freeport pier."

"Right." Frank held on tighter to the side of the boat. "And so will we."

Joe was no longer listening. He maneuvered the speeding boat closer to the racecourse. Ahead, Wills was fighting madly with the cabin cruiser's wheel, trying to avoid a collision.

Jason fired off two more shots. This time one tore a hole into the side of the Hardys' inboard.

"That makes six," Frank shouted. "His gun's empty! Go on, open the throttle all the way!"

Joe sped up and veered to starboard in an effort to force Wills closer to the dangerous lanes of the speed course. Within seconds, both boats had zoomed into the thick of the race. The roar of the high-powered racing engines mingled with their own, drowning out the shouts of the watching crowds.

Frank could see Wills pulling hard to port, cutting across in front of the Hardys. A torrent of water descended on the brothers, momentarily blinding them. By the time Joe had cleared his eyes, the cruiser's bulk was blocking his view of the course ahead.

"Look, he's moving!" Frank shouted.

Joe peered ahead through the flying water as the cabin cruiser moved suddenly to port again.

Now the view ahead was wide and clear. But Joe didn't like what he saw.

"It's coming right at us!" Frank yelled.

Joe's hands tightened on the wheel. A bright red, full-powered racing boat was bearing down on them at over a hundred miles per hour.

They were headed the wrong way down the course!

Joe shot a look over at Frank, then braced himself for the impending crash.

Chapter

17

"HARD TO PORT!" Joe heard Frank shout. Instinctively, he turned the wheel to the left. At the same time Frank grabbed the throttle, slamming it all the way forward.

To Joe's relief, the driver of the approaching racer steered his boat in the opposite direction, and he and the Hardys narrowly cleared each other. In the instant before they were drenched with the racer's spray, Joe could hear the other driver scream in a foreign language.

Poor guy, Joe thought as he realigned his boat. He's lost his chance to win and all because of us.

But Frank intruded on his musings. "Speed it up!" he ordered. "They've almost reached Freeport Harbor!"

Joe hit the throttle again, trying to ignore the jeers from the audience gathered on the beach.

Wills and Jason were just climbing onto shore as the Hardys reached the harbor. Joe switched off the engine, and both boys jumped onto the dock before the boat had even stopped.

"Come on!" Joe yelled as he and Frank raced after the fleeing crooks.

As they reached the end of the dock, Frank made a flying leap and just managed to tackle Wills around the legs and drop him to the ground.

"Atta boy!" Joe grabbed Jason by the collar and spun him around. Without a weapon to back them up, Wills and Jason knew they were no match for the Hardys. As Joe held on to Jason, he heard a helicopter thundering in the distance.

He looked up to see a white harbor patrol chopper headed their way. A red flag hung out the passenger door, fluttering in the wind. "The race must have been called off," Joe said. Then he felt sheepish, realizing it had been their fault.

"That racing boat we almost hit is leading the chopper to us," Frank pointed out. "Gee, do we have any liability insurance?"

Joe sighed resignedly as the helicopter hovered above them and a voice called down via megaphone. "You are all under arrest!"

Joe didn't care that the harbor patrol thought

he and his brother were criminals. He and Frank could explain all that later. The important thing was that Dr. Wills and Jason would be arrested, too.

Two police cars pulled up in a cloud of dust in the parking lot across the way. Joe and Frank waited as three police officers bolted from the cars and approached the dock, their weapons drawn and ready. "Hey, look," Joe said to Frank. "There's our old friend, Sergeant Mylan!"

"You will all raise your hands and remain still," the amplified voice instructed from above.

Seeing that they were covered, Joe let go of Jason while Frank released Dr. Wills. All four of them raised their hands as ordered.

Sergeant Mylan stood on the dock behind the armed officers. At his signal the three uniformed officers charged forward. In scant moments all four men were in handcuffs.

"I guess you two just can't stay out of trouble," Sergeant Mylan said, approaching the Hardys. "Let's retreat to the station and get this all down on paper, shall we?" He led the way to the patrol cars.

Joe gave Jason a big, toothy smile. "With pleasure, Sarge," he crowed.

"That took longer than I thought," Joe admitted four hours later when Sergeant Mylan finally decided he was satisfied with their story and released them. "No hard feelings I hope, Sergeant. In fact, I was wondering if you could meet us on board the *Valiant* tomorrow afternoon? We want to get everyone together and clear up all the mystery."

"I'll be there," the sergeant agreed in his clipped accent. "Frankly, boys, from now on I wouldn't miss a thing you two were involved in."

"Those pirates!" Captain Delaney roared the next day when the Hardys finished unfolding the mystery of the missing treasure to the entire *Valiant* crew. "That explains why Ben Wills insisted he be the only one to deal with the lab reports."

"He lied about the lab findings. The results were actually positive. He also instructed Jason to steer the search off course," Frank explained. "That worked until you got frustrated enough to pilot the ship yourself."

Joe glanced at his fellow crew members, who were seated around the large table in the lounge. He was proud to see none of them had deserted ship despite the past weeks' difficulties. In fact, there were more people than ever on board. Besides Sergeant Mylan, the middle-aged couple whose boat the Hardys had borrowed had accepted the captain's invitation to drop in. They shared in the party atmosphere as the *Valiant* celebrated its release from the criminals' grip.

"Their plan was to define the actual location of the *Doña Bonita* and its treasure with their sonar markers." Joe added. "All they had to do was lead this excursion off course for one more week, when Captain Delaney would run out of funds and be forced into bankruptcy, and then—"

"They'd form their own expedition and claim everything for themselves," Bob finished for him. He looked sheepish. "Sorry I let the cat out of the bag by telling Jason about your plans to visit Waves. It came up in conversation when I asked him if he'd like to go to the races with us."

"That's when he got the idea to set us up with Max Trepo, hoping he could scare us off," Joe said.

"Right," Frank went on. "But Jason got too far ahead of himself when he tried to get some easy cash for one of the artifacts. He thought he could stay in the clear by assuming Peter's identity. That way, if Max got caught fencing it, Peter would be fingered as the source."

"He even registered at that sleazy hotel under Peter's name after Peter had disappeared from the *Valiant*, to make it seem as though he were still alive," Joe said. He glanced nervously at Gina, to whom he'd gently broken the news of Peter's death earlier.

Gina rubbed the ring that Alastair had given her. "My brother found out about their scheme and they killed him." She took a deep breath in order to go on. "Just as they killed Harry Lyman when he found out too much."

Joe nodded sympathetically. "Dr. Wills knew about Harry's heart problems when the kid signed up," he said. "He promised to hide Harry's medical history from Captain Delaney. Harry was probably grateful, not knowing that Wills had done it because he preferred a disposable crew."

"Fortunately, we still have the body," announced Sergeant Mylan. "The coroner is doing a new autopsy now."

"And all the time we thought you two were just a couple of troublemakers!" the middle-aged woman from the dock exclaimed. Joe smiled at her expression and was relieved she wasn't still angry.

"We called the harbor patrol to report that our boat had been stolen by a couple of hoodlums," her husband said ruefully, patting his wife's hand. "We had plans to charge you boys with assault and battery, too—that is, until we found out what was really going on."

Joe felt even guiltier. "I'm really sorry about what happened," he said. "Is there any way we can repay you?"

"Well, the boat has been damaged," the man pointed out.

"No need to worry about that," Captain Delaney said, walking over to the couple. "By next week you'll have a brand-new boat, with my compliments. Without your boat—and the Hardys behind the wheel—Dr. Wills and Jason would be long gone by now."

Joe was relieved to see the woman's face light up again. "Why, thank you," she said. "That's very generous of you."

"Attention, attention," Joe said now, turning back to the crew. "There's another person we have to thank."

He nodded toward Alastair, who sat slumped back in one of the easy chairs. "If it hadn't been for our Bahamian friend here, Captain Delaney would have lost his ship."

"That's right," Frank agreed. "We had to leave him on board to fight the flames alone."

Alastair studied his shoes, embarrassed by all the attention. "It was mainly just burning newspapers. The fire extinguisher did all the work."

"We'll be able to get that hallway in shape by the end of the week," Vic assured the captain. "All it needs is some scraping, a little paint, and a new coat of marine varnish for the woodwork."

Captain Delaney stepped over to Alastair and clasped him around his shoulder. "I'll never be able to thank you enough, Poison, for saving this old rig. It means a lot to me," he said.

Then he moved to Gina and took her hand. "Your brother was a hero," he told her. "I'll see to it that you get his share of the profits as well as your own."

"Thank you," she said. "Yes, he was a hero."

"And last, but certainly not least, all of our thanks to Frank and Joe Hardy. Benjamin Wills couldn't possibly have chosen better!" Captain Delaney grabbed the brothers' arms and raised them above their heads in a gesture of victory as the group enthusiastically applauded.

"You guys are great! Thanks!" Joe said, trying to be modest. He exchanged a triumphant look with his brother, whose grin stretched from ear to ear.

"You know, Frank," he said for everyone's benefit, "if this hasn't been good old-fashioned American fun, I don't know what is!"

Frank and Joe's next case:

Scandal rocks the Bayport police force! New commissioner Mark DeCampo has suspended veteran police chief Ezra Collig, saying he has proof Collig was once a bagman in a bribery scheme. Now Collig is on the run, and when DeCampo barely survives a car bomb, the chief is accused of attempted murder!

The Hardys have had differences with Collig in the past, but they refuse to believe that he's a dirty cop. The boys head to Millerton, the town where Collig began his career, and expose a thirty-five-year-old police cover-up. But they also stir up a new case—a case of deceit, dishonor, and danger that leads straight back to Bayport . . . in *Beyond the Law,* Case #55 in The Hardy Boys Casefiles™.